CHILD
OF
DARK
WATER

A Novella

E.G. RAND

CASTLE BRIDGE MEDIA
DENVER, COLORADO, USA

CASTLE BRIDGE MEDIA
Denver, Colorado

Cover art by Markus Spiske/Unsplash.
This photo has been modified.

This book is a work of fiction. Names, characters, business, events, and incidents are the products of the author's imaginations. Any resemblance to actual persons, living or dead or actual events is purely coincidental.

CHILD OF DARK WATER
© 2025 E.G. Rand
All rights reserved.

ISBN: 979-8-9917855-2-5

CHAPTER ONE

OUTSIDE THE TOWN OF RIDGEWAY, a long fire road led to a gravel lot where an '82 Bronco truck was parked among the tall grasses and weeds. Two men sat in the dark on a run-down wooden dock, fishing poles bobbing in the water and an open cooler between them. Dale Kyler was a heavy-set man. He wore his gray and black hair in a long braid, a dingy baseball cap covering his weathered face.

His cousin Jeff Wright was slumped in the chair next to him, idly scratching at a filthy flannel shirt. Jeff Wright was a lifelong bachelor and layabout. Jeff had lived with Dale in his trailer for the past three months.

This part of the lake had been popular for fishing decades ago but had been forgotten when a new dock was built closer to town. Now the old fishing dock was showing its age, limping into the lake muck and tall reeds of the shoreline. The wooden boards groaned threateningly beneath his deck chair as Dale dug for another brew from the cooler.

"You see those missing posters all over town?" asked Dale.

"Yep," Jeff grunted, lighting a cigarette. "Can't go anywhere without seeing Amber Prenley."

Dale clucked his tongue.

"Poor girl. I went to school with her mother, Gloria. Amber seemed like a nice kid."

"We ain't sure she's dead," said Jeff. "Sheriff Breeson thinks she ran off with the baby's father."

Dale snorted, cracking a beer.

"Sheriff Breeson couldn't find his ass with two hands and a map. That girl was eight months pregnant and bedridden with preeclampsia. Amber couldn't have run away if she wanted to."

Jeff had no idea what preeclampsia was, but he didn't ask. Dale was sensitive about that sort of thing– his wife died in childbirth in '93 and the baby along with her. Dale had never been the same.

The two men sat in silence for a long moment.

"Something's in the water over there." Jeff gestured to a nearby spot in the lake. A dark mass lay beneath the water's surface, almost matte in the moonlight. "Looks like algae bloom, or something rotting."

Dale grunted as he lit a cigarette with his favorite lighter. Just as Dale clicked the zippo shut, a noise came off the lake. It was a high, mewling sound, distinctly animal in nature. At first Dale thought it was a coyote or a cat. He cocked his head, listening.

"You hear that?" he hissed towards Jeff. Jeff shook his head.

It sounded again, closer now. The noise made the hair on the back of Dale's neck stand up. It was not an animal sound, he realized– it was a human sound.

The crying of a baby.

Dale jumped to his feet. "You really don't hear that?" The noise got louder and louder in the wind. Dale felt his heart hammer in his chest with each pitiful cry.

"You sure it's not a bobcat or something?" asked Jeff, "You know, my father used to say a bobcat in heat sounded just like–"

Dale was not listening. He had run towards the shore, looking into the water for the source of the sound.

"I can't see shit out here!" he grumbled.

"What are you doin?" shouted Jeff. "Goddammit, Dale, what are you on about?"

Dale stumbled back to the truck for light. The crying had become more insistent. Dale had spent a lot of his life by this lake, and he'd never heard a sound like that.

But all the beer was catching up to him, and after tossing his phone and wallet onto the floorboards, it took Dale a few tries to get his key into the truck's ignition. He stood by the truck and turned on the Broncos lights, sending two yellow cones peering into the lake by the dock.

"Dale!" hollered Jeff, alarm making his voice even twangier. "Dale, what the hell you–"

Dale shushed him. After he set the lights he stood next to the car, head cocked, listening.

The sound was coming from the shoreline, emanating from a clump of reeds just outside of the truck's lights. Dale's mind swam with animal sympathy. The panicked cry of a baby, choked with pain and alarm, was almost too much to bear. He stumbled away from the truck towards the lake as fast as his sobriety would allow.

"I hear something!" Dale pushed past Jeff, who had gotten off of the dock in a half-hearted attempt to stop his cousin.

Jeff figured it was best to just let this episode play out. He leaned against the hood of the truck, swigging from his beer and watching as Dale ran into the lake.

The shoreline at this part of the lake was not as solid as it looked. The water was very deep, and the bank was layered with decades of leaves from the surrounding trees. Dale was up to his chest almost immediately, unseen animals slithered past his legs in the black water. Above him, trees reached out branches like skeletal hands, prepared to push Dale into the lake's darkest depths.

The crying was more insistent than ever, calling him further and further from shore, just outside of the halo of headlights. Dale did not stop to think about how a small child could have found themselves caught in the reeds of such a remote area of the lake, nor did he consider the strong smell of rot coming off of the water. He plunged forward, the mud pulling at his boots as he pushed towards the source of the sound.

But it wasn't just mud pulling at Dale's legs. Something was wrapping itself around Dale's ankles, as deft and deadly as a viper. The crying turned to a howl; it seemed that the child was in mortal pain. Dale reached for the reeds and Jeff tried again to coax him back.

"Come on now, Dale, You're being—" Jeff's voice caught in his throat.

In the blink of an eye, something dark and slick slipped up from the surface of the lake. It covered Dale, pulling him under the water in a single pulse. One moment Dale was there, the next moment he was gone. There was no splashing or flailing, no call for help. Just the rippling black lake under the moonlight, and Jeff's echoing screams.

CHAPTER TWO

SHERIFF BREESON SAT WITH HIS heels on his desk, drinking his coffee (two sugar, two cream) and reading the morning paper. Sunbeams sliced through the surrounding forest, burning away the comforting mist of night. It was going to be another hot day in Ridgeway.

The Sheriff was too old for the night shift, but he still took it once a week. With only two officers at the station he had no choice. Now he was ending his night shift the exact same way he had for the past fourteen years, and neither the presence of a new officer nor the caterwauling from the drunk tank was going to stop him today. Ridgeway was his kingdom, and here Derrick Breeson was the king. It helped that the small lakeside community had almost no crime.

The door swung open and the new transfer to the Police Department walked in. Alice Goodwin had been working in the town for four months, which was still considered new for Ridgeway.

"Why is Jeff Wright in the cell?" she asked. Sheriff Breeson dropped the newspaper, looking into Goodwin's gray eyes. She was a tall, broad-shouldered woman with a hard face and thick blonde hair, which she wore in a bun. Officer Goodwin did nothing to hide the severe burn scars that ran up the right side of her neck, disfiguring her ear and part of her right cheek. They were painful to look at.

"Drunk and disorderly" Grunted Breeson, "He came in here last night, reeking of beer and raving about some monster by the old dock. I put him in the drunk tank to cool off."

A plaintive wail came from the station's single jail cell.

"Please! Somethin' terrible has happened to Dale!"

Officer Goodwin raised her eyebrows at Sheriff Breeson.

"Dale Kyler, Jeff's cousin. He probably got drunk and wandered off."

"Probably?" Said Goodwin.

Sheriff Breeson snapped his paper shut, getting heavily to his feet. He was too old to deal with damaged goods like Alice Goodwin. She was too much of a city cop, hardheaded and stubborn. He wished they had sent him someone more tractable, a nice family man.

"I am going home, Officer Goodwin," Breeson said, gathering his hat and cigarettes. "You are welcome to question the local drunks all you like."

Officer Goodwin struggled to not let contempt show on her face. In a measured voice she asked, "Any news on the Prenley case?"

"Nope," grunted the Sheriff. "And there won't be. Amber Prenley ran away with the father of her baby."

"Well, I am going to drop by the Prenley place today and see if Gloria Prenley remembers anything else that could help us."

The Sheriff gave her a shrug that said *while away the hours however you like* before tipping his hat to Goodwin and seeing himself out.

CHAPTER THREE

AFTER SHERIFF BREESON'S TAIL LIGHTS disappeared from the parking lot, Goodwin let Jeff Wright out of the station's holding cell. The heat of the day rose as Officer Goodwin got Jeff a cup of coffee and asked him what happened.

Jeff Wright was something of a frequent flier at the Ridgeway Police Station. Nothing serious—public intoxication, DUI, the occasional petty theft, or possession. Jeff Wright always looked bad at the police station, but he looked worse today. Frail, agitated, jumping at every small sound. Officer Goodwin listened as Jeff recounted the night's events in a shaking voice.

"I'm telling the truth," Jeff groaned, head in his hands. "Something came up out of the lake and *got* Dale. Sucked him right under the surface of the water. He never came back up."

"Did you get a good look at what it was?"

"I didn't. It all happened so fast…. Dale said he heard a sound, he went into the water to investigate, and then he was gone."

"What did he hear?" asked Goodwin, taking notes.

"I have no idea!" cried Jeff, "He just kept saying he heard something. The next thing I knew he was in the water…"

"Did you try to go in after him?" asked Goodwin.

"No," said Jeff. He looked at Officer Goodwin with shameful, bloodshot eyes. "I was afraid."

Goodwin didn't need a lie detector to see that he was telling the truth.

Jeff Wright looked scared shitless. But he also had stale beer coming out of his pores, and Goodwin found it hard to believe that this incident wasn't alcohol-related.

The ancient Bronco Jeff had driven was parked across three spots in the station's small lot, no doubt left there by a panicked and hammered Mr. Wright. He was lucky he hadn't killed anyone on the trip from the dock to the station.

Goodwin told him as much when she let him go. She marched Jeff into the sunshine, walking out from the cool shelter of the station into a wall of heat and humidity.

"I am sure your cousin Dale is at home right now," Goodwin said in a tone she hoped was congenial. "I bet you'll find him on the couch, hungover and mad that he had to walk home."

In the light of the bright summer day Jeff looked even worse than he had in the drunk tank. He seemed to have aged a decade overnight—his hair was gray, his face pressed and colorless. He pulled a loose cigarette out of his breast pocket and lit it with shaking hands before saying, "Officer, something in that lake killed my cousin. And I intend to go out and find Dale's body, with or without your help."

Goodwin sighed. A force inside of her, something between intuition and curiosity, swayed her resolve. "Alright. How about this—if Dale isn't at home when you get there, call the station and leave a message. I've got some work to do, but I'll check the machine after lunch. If I have a message from you, I'll go down to where you guys were fishing and see if I find anything."

"You'll see me there," said Jeff, before he turned and walked to the truck. Goodwin watched him go, a strange feeling in the pit of her stomach. She had not worked in Ridgeway for long, but she had become well acquainted with Jeff Wright. He was a drunk, but he wasn't a liar.

And if he was telling the truth, that meant there wasn't one missing person in this town, but two. The Amber Prenley case was already keeping her up at night…a beautiful young girl, heavily pregnant, had disappeared into thin air. No evidence, no witnesses, scant few suspects. She didn't need another case like that.

Officer Goodwin checked her watch. She had told Gloria Prenley that she would be at her home at quarter to nine, which meant she had to leave the station within the next twenty minutes. Alice Goodwin was nothing if not punctual.

13

CHAPTER FOUR

JEFF DIDN'T BOTHER CHECKING THE trailer. He got back into the Bronco and headed straight for the old dock, his mind a bee's nest of panic. Jeff was kicking himself for thinking the damn police would help him. If he was going to find out what happened to Dale, he was going to have to do it alone.

As he navigated the Bronco back to last night's fishing spot. He parked the car and lit another cigarette, trying to calm his nerves. He looked around him—dense forest and shimmering lake water, bathed in sunlight. Somehow that didn't make the scene any less threatening. Jeff reached into the glove box and wrapped his hand around the cool handle of a 686 Smith & Wesson.

Whatever got Dale was going to have to work a little harder to get him.

He slid out of the truck, squinting in the light of day. His head swam from the light dancing across the placid lake water, the titter of songbirds in the trees. The Bronco had no A/C and Jeff was already soaked in sweat. He could see the tire impressions of where he'd left the night before, deep furrows in the gravel and upturned dirt.

Everything was just as he and Dale had left it. On the rickety dock the cooler sat between two old deck chairs, fishing poles still bobbing in the water. It was eerie, as if the scene from the night before had patiently waited for him to return.

Jeff's head throbbed, and his pulse pounded in his ears. He felt like he was moving through cement. The day was getting hotter and more humid as Jeff tried to straighten his thoughts. He retraced the steps from the night before.

They had been on the dock, and then Dale had run off to the car. Jeff remembered Dale hanging out of the Bronco's door, listening, before diving into the water of the lake. Jeff walked up the shore alongside the dock, to the sandy line that marked the descent into the water. A breeze caused thick reeds to rustle against the dock like a snake rattle. Jeff looked down into the murky water. It was deep here, deeper than it looked. The water was still, full of slimy, nasty things that lived in the sludge of the bank.

The wind changed, and Jeff was assaulted by a terrible smell. A lifelong hunter, Jeff knew the aroma of animal decomposition. Something was putrefying nearby, the smell so strong that he nearly gagged. He put his hands on his knees, suddenly faint. In his ears he heard a ringing sound, and then something else– something stranger.

A baby crying.

Jeff straightened up. He heard it again, a baby crying. It was coming from the end of the dock as if a child had gotten stuck in the water and couldn't get out. The sound made no sense all the way out here. The hair on the back of his neck stood as he looked, trying to find the source of the sound.

The crying became louder, mixed with frantic coughing, like a child drowning. Jeff, with the smell of death still lingering in his nose and his hand on his gun, rushed down the old dock. The boards screamed in protest with each heavy footfall. Jeff tried not to look at the chairs and cooler as he passed.

He stopped at the edge of the dock, looking for the source of the crying. The noise had suddenly stopped when Jeff approached. He looked around for a boat or splashing. Then he stared directly down into the water and screamed.

There, just below the surface, floated the body of a human baby boy. It looked like a newborn, perfectly formed but definitely dead. Jeff could see the delicate blue webbing of the veins in the child's eyes, its full mouth, small hands curled to his face as if it had just drifted into a peaceful slumber.

Jeff was transfixed and then snapped out of it—he got down on his knees, tossing the gun aside to try to fish the child out of the water. The baby looked like he had just slipped under, and Jeff hoped there was still a chance to revive him.

The moment Jeff's fingers grazed the water, the infant's eyes snapped open. Jeff screamed for a second time. Beneath the child's eyelids was nothing, nothing but churning black mud. A slick black tendril, like a lamprey eel, slipped from the water and wrapped itself around Jeff's arm, tightening a vise-like grip. With one fluid movement, Jeff Wright was yanked into the lake.

Jeff grasped at the dock, managing to grab one of the old boards. He thrashed against the creature that pulled him. He screamed, kicking and flailing. A second tendril emerged from the water, wrapping itself around Jeff Wright's neck, squeezing until a loud pop rang out, followed by the crunch of bone. Jeff Wright let go of the dock, and his body sank beneath the surface of the dirty water.

CHAPTER FIVE

OFFICER GOODWIN NAVIGATED HER CRUISER to the Prenley house. In her short time here, Goodwin had gotten a good lay of the land. The town of Ridgeway was shaped like an inverted triangle, with one side bordered by Lake Munahegan.

The Prenleys lived off of Old Dairy Road, inland from the lake, in a working-class suburb. Not mansions like the Lakeshore community, but not as impoverished as the Pineville Trailer Park, where anger and resentment hung in the air as thick as smoke. Officer Goodwin got a lot of calls from Pineville.

She parked her car in front of Gloria Prenley's home– a modest two-story surrounded by carefully tended flower beds. Goodwin steeled herself for the interaction. Gloria Prenley had been helpful in the beginning, but as the weeks dragged on she was becoming frustrated by the inaction of the police department. It was only a matter of time before Gloria decided that the cops couldn't—or wouldn't—help her.

Goodwin rang the doorbell and stood back, hat in hand. Upon closer inspection, the flower beds around the home were overgrown and choked with weeds. She figured that it was hard to focus on gardening when your daughter and unborn grandchild had been missing for almost a month.

Gloria Prenley opened the door. She was a sturdy, attractive woman in her early fifties with closely cropped dyed blonde hair and bright blue eyes, which Amber had inherited. Goodwin noticed the bags beneath Gloria's eyes, the lines pressed around her mouth. Gloria Prenley looked like the picture of worry.

"Have you heard anything?" Asked Gloria after Goodwin accepted her invitation for a cup of coffee, sitting at a small table in the kitchen. Even though it was a sunny morning the house was dark. The blinds were drawn, and the air still. It was as if the house was holding its breath.

"We haven't," sighed Goodwin. "But I was hoping I could ask you a few more–"

"I knew it. You aren't even trying to find her," wailed Gloria.

"Ms. Prenley, I *promise* I am trying to find your daughter, but we just don't have enough information to go on yet. Are you sure you have no idea who the father of her baby was? Amber didn't have any boyfriends, male friends, acquaintances? Anything?"

Gloria threw up her hands in frustration. "The million-dollar question! I am telling you, officer, if I knew who knocked up my daughter, I would be banging down his door right now! My Amber had no interest in boys. When she came home pregnant you could have knocked me down with a feather." Gloria's rage dissolved into grief as tears smudged her thick eyeliner. She got up and retrieved two mugs of coffee. When she returned, she continued in a defeated voice.

"You have to understand, officer, my girl….she would never just leave. She wasn't like that. I raised Amber on my own. It had just been the two of us for as long as I can remember. She would have never run off and not said anything."

This was a line that Goodwin often got from parents of runaways. But when she looked at Gloria, intuition told her the woman was being truthful. Amber really was not the kind of girl to run off.

"Were you angry about Amber's pregnancy? Maybe she thought–"

"No, no." Gloria waved the idea away. "I mean sure, I was mad at first. She knew how we struggled when she was young. I had wanted better for her. I was frustrated that she wouldn't tell me who the father was, at least for child support. But I wasn't angry. I wanted that grandbaby. Besides, Amber didn't have enough money to strike out on her own. I checked her bank account after she disappeared, and she had 300 bucks to her name."

This was new information. Amber's phone had gone missing with her, and they had been unable to find anything on the phone records that could help them. In addition, she appeared to be the only teenager in the world who did not post constantly on social media, so they found no clues there either. But a bank account could reveal a paper trail of some kind.

"Has any money left that account since she went missing?" Asked Goodwin eagerly, but Gloria sighed and shook her head.

"No, no money coming in or out."

They sat in tense silence. Both of the women knew that teenage runaways do not let money sit in their bank accounts.

"Maybe she had cash?" Pondered Gloria, grasping at straws. "She did get paid in cash when she babysat."

For the second time, Officer Goodwin perked up.

"You didn't tell me she babysat." She said as she scribbled in her notes,

Gloria furrowed her brow. "I thought I told you. Amber babysat for Hunter and Tabby Wellworth in Lakeshore. I've cleaned houses in Lakeshore for the past fifteen years. The money is good enough that I could do that while Amber was at school and be there when she got home. I cleaned Grant Wellworth's house for five years and he liked me so much that when Hunter moved out, I cleaned for them too…"

Despite her grief, Goodwin could hear the pride in Gloria's voice. The Wellworths were a well-known name in the sleepy town, a wealthy family who owned a local chain of banks. Grant Wellworth and Sheriff Breeson went golfing together almost every Sunday.

"How did Amber get the job at the Wellworths?" asked Goodwin.

Gloria furrowed her brow, thinking. Finally she said, "When I was cleaning there last summer, Hunter's wife, Tabby, asked if I knew any good babysitters for their two little boys, Tanner and Jay. So I recommended Amber. After that she was over there all the time… she loved kids, Amber did. She loved those boys." Gloria's voice trailed off, thinking about her happy, pregnant daughter. A rooster shaped clock ticked in the dark kitchen.

"Do you think I could take a look in her room?" asked Goodwin gently.

Gloria seemed deflated, done with the interview. She nodded to Goodwin's request and silently led her up the stairs of the house. The place was crowded, hot and stuffy.

As they ascended the carpeted stairs Goodwin looked at all the pictures hanging on the wall. Amber as a baby wearing a huge pink bow, Gloria and toddler Amber swimming in a pool that matched their bright eyes. Amber holding up a lizard in the Florida Keys. Goodwin had investigated her fair share of runaways, and they rarely came from such loving homes. Goodwin wondered if Sheriff Breeson had even bothered to talk to Gloria before declaring her daughter a runaway.

The door to Amber's room was white and decorated with pastel flowers. Gloria unlocked the door and pushed it open. She turned her face away as she did so, as if avoiding a bad smell.

"I can't go in there," she said, voice catching "I haven't been able to go in since she…"

"It's okay," said Goodwin, cutting her off. "You can wait downstairs if you like. This will only take a minute."

Gloria nodded and rushed back down the steps. Goodwin flipped on the light, illuminating a small bedroom with a white twin bed, a white desk and a matching bedside table. The walls had old-fashioned white and pink wallpaper laced with roses, and white lace curtains were pulled over the window. Goodwin thought the room looked like it belonged to a little girl, not a teenager. The only stark exception was the bassinet, which was set up by the window, ready for the arrival of Amber's child.

Goodwin started at the small desk adorned with glass unicorn ornaments, above which Amber had proudly stuck her most recent report card– mostly A's. On the desk was a teal wallet. Goodwin donned a pair of gloves and opened the wallet, where she found Amber's driver's license and bank cards, as well as over fifty dollars in small bills.

She inwardly groaned. Another thing runaways didn't leave behind was their ID.

Goodwin checked the rest of the desk and, finding nothing, went to the twin bed which was made up with a white lacy duvet and an enormous pile of pillows. Her mother had said that Amber had severe preeclampsia and was mostly bedridden by the time she went missing. She had spent a lot of her time reading.

On the nightstand next to the bed was an open jewelry box, the kind with a mirror and a twirling ballerina, containing a few pieces of costume jewelry. Next to that was a small pile of books about childbirth and motherhood, including a book of baby names. Goodwin noticed that Amber had bookmarked a few pages. There was also a bottle of prenatal vitamins and a glass of water fuzzy with dust.

Goodwin got down on her knees in front of the bed and checked underneath. She found a neat row of shoes with one set conspicuously missing. This tracked with Gloria's statement that, when she went missing, Amber only wore green rubber crocs because they were easy to slip on, and nothing else fit her swollen feet.

Rocking back on her ankles, Goodwin listed what she knew. Amber had taken her phone and put on her shoes, which meant that she had probably left of her own volition. But she had left behind her ID and money. To Goodwin, that meant she intended to come back. After all, Amber's mother claimed that she couldn't stand or even sit up for long periods, and her baby was due in just a few weeks.

Goodwin got to her feet and was about to leave when something prompted her to check Amber's jewelry box on her nightstand.

She took out a small flashlight to look through the pieces, the majority of which were the kind of things owned by all teenage girls– tangled gold and silver chains, fake pearl earrings, random coins. But as she combed through, Goodwin noticed that there was another chamber beneath the jewelry box– the perfect place to put something you wanted to hide. Goodwin pulled open the hiding spot to reveal a gold and emerald ring.

Goodwin held the ring up to the light. She was no expert, but it looked expensive. The gem glittered, and the band appeared to be real gold. It was not something Amber could afford on her own. She flipped the ring over to reveal an inscription on the inside of the band.

AP & HW

Goodwin's face broke into a sneer, pulling down the scar tissue that ran along her neck. Amber Prenley was obviously AP, and after talking to Gloria,

Goodwin had a pretty good idea of who HW was.

When she came downstairs Goodwin confirmed with Gloria that Amber did not own any expensive jewelry. Then Officer Goodwin thanked her for her time and left, taking the ring in an evidence bag with her. She had a feeling it would come in handy where she was going next.

CHAPTER SIX

HUNTER AND TABITHA WELLWORTH'S HOME could not be more different than the Prenley's. There was no darkness there. The two-story lake house featured massive floor to ceiling windows that overlooked Lake Munahegan. The classical home was filled with resplendent light– from its exposed beam ceiling to its polished wood floors, illuminating the tasteful furniture in various shades of white. The back lawn was surrounded by woodland and sloped down to the Wellworths private dock and small navy of fishing boats and yachts.

Tabitha, Tabby to her many friends, sat in the afternoon sun and scrolled through her phone. In the distance she could hear her two boys, Jay and Tanner, bickering and wailing in the playroom. She was just considering sneaking some vodka into her water bottle when the doorbell rang. Tabby went to answer it and was shocked to find a horribly burned female police officer on her doorstep.

Officer Goodwin introduced herself and asked if Hunter was around. Tabby said that he wasn't, but that he was due home at any moment. Goodwin observed Tabitha Wellworth carefully. She was a petite, frail looking woman in her early forties. She had wide, honey-colored eyes in a doll's face, surrounded by masses of mahogany hair. In her designer clothes and diamond rings, Tabby Wellworth was every bit the wealthy housewife.

Tabby invited Goodwin inside to wait for her husband. Goodwin agreed, accepting both a seat at the kitchen island and a carbonated water from Tabby. Goodwin watched out of the corner of her eye as Tabby seated herself opposite, trying not to stare at the burn scar that covered Goodwin's neck and ear.

"Can I ask what you need to speak to Hunter about?" asked Tabby. Even her voice seemed fragile, like a bird.

"I'm investigating Amber Prenley's disappearance. I know that she babysat for you, I just wanted to ask your husband if he knew of anyone who would want to do her harm."

"Oh dear," said Tabby, her voice heavy, "Of course. Poor Amber. My boys, Tanner and Jay, have been just beside themselves. Amber was more of a nanny than a babysitter. She stayed with them after school a few times a week, sometimes overnight in the guest suite."

From the other corner of the mansion there was a loud crash and an angry howl, presumably from the boys Tabby was talking about. She appeared not to hear it.

"Did she ever talk to you about having a boyfriend? Ever catch her sneaking someone into the house?"

"Amber would never!" Tabby sounded scandalized. "I am sure she must have had a beau, seeing as she was in the family way. But she never said anything to me about it."

The din of bickering and screaming had moved to where the two women sat. Goodwin looked up to see two small boys tumble into the kitchen. The taller of the two, a brick of a boy with flaming red hair, sat on top of the smaller boy, who was brunette and had Tabby's honey-colored eyes. They both looked to be under ten, the redhead being larger and older. They were fighting viciously on the marble floor, screaming bloody murder.

"Boys, stop fighting," sighed Tabby. The redheaded boy ignored her, raising his hand to smack his brother again when he noticed Officer Goodwin glaring at them from the kitchen table.

"EWWW!" Screamed the boy, jumping to his feet and pointing at Goodwin, "What's wrong with your ear! You look like a monster!"

Goodwin stared at the two children, unfazed. Tabby gave the officer a wincing, apologetic look.

"Officer Goodwin is here to help look for Amber," said Tabby in a strange, sticky sweet voice.

"Daddy says she's not coming back," piped up the other little boy, who had scrambled to his feet and was standing a safe distance away from his brother.

"And why's that?" asked Goodwin casually. The boy looked nervous, as if he had done something wrong.

"Shut up, Jay!" Tanner screamed, lunging again and grabbing the smaller boy around the throat.

"Now Tanner, be nice," said Tabby in the same strange, soothing tone.

Fearing that the boy might strangle his brother unconscious, Goodwin shouted at him to knock it off.

At this the room fell silent.

Tabby glared at Officer Goodwin as Tanner ran to his mother like a frightened calf. Mother and son clutched each other, looking gobsmacked.

Goodwin turned back to the other little boy, Jay, who was rubbing his neck. Goodwin helped him to his feet and asked him what his father told him about Amber.

"He said she ran away to get married," Jay said, staring at his shoes as he spoke. "Daddy said that Amber moved really far away and that we would never see her again."

"Did he tell you exactly where she went?" Asked Goodwin, and Jay bit his lip, shaking his head.

"No, he just said we would never see her again." Jay's voice was so full of sadness that Goodwin felt it in her heart. She wondered how many times Amber had saved Jay from his older brother.

"What is going on here?"

An angry voice cut through the air. Goodwin turned to see a glaring, well-dressed man in the doorway. He was a larger version of the redheaded boy, with a chiseled white face that women who like golfing would consider handsome. His hair was the same fire engine red as Tanner's. Goodwin knew him immediately to be Hunter Wellworth, first born son of Grant Wellworth and the master of the house.

"Daddy!" Screamed Tanner, who immediately dropped his mother to run to his father, throwing his arms around his neck and feverishly kissing his face. Goodwin figured the boy to be too old for such histrionics. His father absently swatted his son aside.

"Who are you?" He demanded of Goodwin, "What are you doing in my house?"

Officer Goodwin introduced herself and told them that she was looking for information about Amber.

"Why ask me?" snapped Hunter.

"Your wife told me she babysat for you," replied Goodwin. "I thought you might know something that can help us find her."

Hunter Wellworth shot his wife a withering look before turning back to Goodwin.

"Lots of people work for us," said Hunter bluntly. "Amber helped with childcare, yes. But I have no idea where she went. It seems obvious to me that she ran off with the father of her child—"

"The father certainly could be involved in her disappearance." Goodwin's shark gray eyes bore into Hunter Wellworth.

"Listen, officer," said Hunter, a thin veneer of calm, "you're new in town, so I'm going to let this slide. But I want you to know that I do not appreciate the tone you're taking with me, and I certainly do not appreciate you dropping by unannounced to harass my wife and children without me present. Now, please leave, and do not bother my family with this nonsense again."

Goodwin glanced at Tabby, who was carefully studying her hands on the marble countertop. From behind his father's back, Tanner stuck his tongue out at Goodwin before scurrying away. Jay had disappeared when his father arrived.

Accepting defeat, Goodwin followed Hunter to the front door and out of his house. The cold blast of A/C mixed with heat as Goodwin stepped out. Just as Hunter was about to close the door Goodwin turned around.

"One more thing, Mr. Wellworth," said Goodwin. Hunter stood in the open door, glaring, as Goodwin reached into her front pocket and retrieved an evidence bag containing the ring she had found in Amber's bedroom. She dangled the bag in front of Hunter's red face. "Does this look familiar to you?"

She didn't have to ask—the look on Hunter's face said it all. Genuine surprise, recognition, and fear. Goodwin didn't have any real evidence, but she knew she had a suspect.

She smiled broadly.

Hunter slammed the door in her face. She carefully pocketed the evidence bag and walked across the manicured lawn towards her patrol car. She could hear the waves lapping on the lake behind her, and birds singing in the surrounding forest. With all the noise she barely heard the whispering coming from a nearby topiary.

"Psst. Mrs. Cop Lady," hissed a bush at the edge of the Wellworth's driveway. Glancing around, Goodwin ducked down to find Jay Wellworth sitting inside of the bush, perched on a branch like a songbird. Goodwin looked at Jay's strained face and knew he had something he wanted to tell her.

"I don't think Amber is gone," he whispered.

"No? Why not?"

"I *see* her," Jay whispered. "At night."

"You see Amber? Like in the house? Is someone keeping her somewhere?"

But Jay shook his head. "No. I see Amber on the lake." He pointed towards the water, rippling under the cloudless sky. Jay looked at Goodwin, his eyes filled with heavy sadness. The look of a child telling an adult something they could never, would never, believe.

"You mean you see her swimming in the lake?"

Jay shook his head again. "No. She only shows up late at night, with these strange floating lights. She looks different—her face is all white and she's wrapped up in a big black slimy thing. She stands at the end of the dock and stares at the house but… but her feet don't touch the water."

Goodwin, not sure what to make of this statement, thanked Jay for talking to her. It was nearly lunch time, and she had other cases to work on. She got into her cruiser and drove back to the station.

From the lake one could see Hunter Wellworth, standing in his great picture window, staring out at the water. On the surface he looked like a man in repose– a cocktail in one hand, wearing a fresh golfing outfit. But his face was furrowed with deep wrinkles, lines crossing his brow like ripples on the lake. He stared out at the water, swirling with anxiety, drinking his whiskey sour. And from the murky, dark water, something stared back.

28

CHAPTER SEVEN

GOODWIN DECIDED TO STOP FOR lunch at the diner before going back to the office. Wrangler Diner was a popular spot with the locals, run by longtime Ridgeway resident Edith Wrangler and her daughter Sherry. Sherry's husband, Jose, ran the grill in the back. The diner itself was an outdated, run down establishment, but the food was delicious. It was also a great place to learn the local gossip.

Sherry Wrangler, a pleasant, plump woman with an infectious laugh, waited on her personally. Goodwin ordered her usual– a tuna fish sandwich with chips and a black coffee. As she ate, she listened to the conversation around her.

"He would never just leave like that." The mellow tones of Jim Weaver, the owner of the gas station, floated over.

"Dale was as reliable as clockwork, no matter how bad he was drinking. He never missed a shift. Now he misses three in a row? Something ain't right. I tried to tell Sheriff Breeson, but he gave me the brush-off."

"Don't surprise me. All the cops out here are morons."

The second voice belonged to Clarence Hall, and Goodwin could almost feel the comment aimed at her back. She declined to turn around. Clarence Hall was a fat, truculent man and another frequent flier at the Ridgeway Police Station. Mostly drunk and disorderly with the occasional bar fight. Goodwin figured that Jim must be really worried about Dale to talk to Clarence about it.

"I bet that witch did something to him. She's always lurking around that part of the lake. Damn foreigner, wish she would go back to her own country…"

"The witch of the lake ain't no foreigner," snapped Sherry across the counter. "She's Asian, not that I expect your dumb ass to know the difference."

This comment caused a flurry of laughter from the diner. Goodwin allowed herself a peek over her shoulder at Clarence's furious expression. As she did so, someone spoke on her deaf side. It was Harold Spell, the owner of the local hardware store, who had come in and sat down during the altercation.

"Witch of the lake has been here since I was a kid," said Harold ponderously. "If she's a foreigner, then we all are."

"I thought this was a private conversation," grumbled Clarence. He slammed some money down on the table and stormed out, leaving a trail of cigarette smoke and BO in his wake.

"Has she ever hurt someone before?" Goodwin turned to face Harold, a stately man in his late fifties with thick gray hair. Before Harold could answer, Sherry jumped in.

"That's nonsense. The witch don't hurt anyone. She's just a crazy old hermit. "

"Most people never see her," said Harold as he accepted a cup of coffee from Sherry. "She keeps to herself. Rumor has it that her ancestors came here to build the railroad. Some people believe she's over a hundred years old."

Goodwin raised her eyebrows and Harold let out a little laugh.

"All rumors, of course. These small towns do like to talk. Speaking of which, any news on Dale Kyler?"

Goodwin sighed. "I wouldn't know. Breeson is on that case."

"Oh," responded Harold flatly. "Well then, it will probably never get solved. Breeson only cares about the richies and the tourists in Lakeshore."

Goodwin gave him a look that said *I can neither confirm nor deny the validity of that statement.* She paid for her meal, tipping Sherry generously. As she walked back to her car, she pondered the witch of the lake. It was probably true that, if she existed at all, she was just a harmless woman. But it was close to a lead.

As she got into the car her radio buzzed and Sheriff Breeson's voice, heavy with rage, demanded that she return to the police station at once. Bracing herself, Goodwin drove off into the hot afternoon.

31

CHAPTER EIGHT

"WHAT DO YOU MEAN, I'M off the Prenley case?" Goodwin glared across the desk at Sheriff Breeson, who matched her flinty gaze with his own from under his cowboy hat. His downturned liver lips looked almost comical as he placed his calloused hands on the desk before him. When he spoke it was in measured tones of restrained anger.

"I have been getting complaints about you pestering the Wellworths."

"Pestering? I was investigating a missing child! Amber Prenley was weeks away from giving birth and bedridden before she vanished. Isn't that something we should be asking questions about?"

Breeson responded, "I got a call from Hunter Wellworth that said that you smacked his eldest son across the face."

Goodwin nearly laughed until she realized that the Sheriff was serious. She stared at her boss, fair eyebrows disappearing into her hairline.

"Well," snorted Goodwin, "do *you* think I did that?" She placed her own hands on the desk, lowering to face Sheriff Breeson eye to eye, her burns pink and glistening in the light as she spoke. "Do you think that I, in the pursuit of finding Amber Prenley, slapped an elementary schooler across the face in front of his mother and security cameras? Do you believe that, Sheriff Breeson?"

"Please sit down, Officer Goodwin," grumbled the Sheriff. She sat and Breeson reclined in his great leather desk chair. It was an ergonomic chair, very expensive. Goodwin considered that Grant Wellworth probably bought him that chair.

"So, Hunter Wellworth is immune to questioning because you play golf with his daddy?" Goodwin couldn't stop herself. Sheriff Breeson shot her a filthy look before saying.

"No one is above the law in Ridgeway. But it's no secret that the Wellworths are a big name, both for this town and for me personally. So if you think that you have found some connection between Hunter Wellworth and Amber Prenley's disappearance, you better have evidence to back it up."

"If you look at the evidence—" Goodwin started.

The Sheriff waved her away. "A ring with some initials won't cut it. There are a lot of HWs out there. No, I would need real evidence. But right now, you don't need to concern yourself with that. I am going to take the lead on Amber Prenley's disappearance—"

Goodwin gritted her teeth as she watched Breeson shove Amber's file into a drawer, crammed with a dozen more just like it. He then placed another file on the desk and slid it over to Officer Goodwin. He smiled as he spoke.

"Since you have time on your hands to chase missing persons, how about you work on this. You remember Jeff Wright, coming in here the other day, yammering on about Dale Kyler being missing?"

Goodwin said that she did. She thought of the locals down at Wranglers diner, and she realized that she had never heard back from Jeff about whether or not Dale was okay.

"Well, the landlady, Mrs. Sims, dropped by Dale's trailer the other night to pick up rent and neither Jeff nor Dale was to be seen. She said it looked like they had been gone a while, their car was missing. Mrs. Sims has been calling me night and day saying that something terrible must have happened to the two of them. Apparently, Dale hasn't missed rent once in the years that he lived there. So, I figured I would put you on the case."

Sheriff Breeson was sticking Goodwin with what he considered to be a shit job, but Goodwin felt a strange tinge in the pit of her stomach. First Amber goes missing, then Dale, and maybe even Jeff Wright. Sheriff Breeson obviously thought that Dale and Jeff had taken off somewhere, trying their luck in another town. But Officer Goodwin remembered how Jeff had looked that day at the police station. He had said he was scared, and she believed him. Now she wondered if they did not have just one missing person, but three.

CHAPTER NINE

THE NEXT DAY ROSE AS hot and bright as the one before. It found Officer Alice Goodwin driving down the long stretch of fire road that led to Dale Kyler and Jeff Wright's favorite fishing spot.

She navigated the charger under the shade of the shifting trees, bright flashes of light coming off the lake. Goodwin wished she could enjoy the area's bucolic beauty, but she couldn't. Her mind swirled with half-formed theories. She was sure that Hunter Wellworth had something to do with Amber's disappearance, but much as she hated to admit it, Sheriff Breeson was right. With no evidence, all she had was a theory about one of the most powerful men in town.

Now Jeff and Dale had gone missing, and Goodwin was starting to wonder if she had gotten this all wrong. What about the woman she had heard them talking about at the diner? The witch of the lake? Goodwin had searched the files for anything about transients in the area, but aside from Jeff Wright nothing came up. Jeff was known to leave town for weeks at a time for work. His cousin, Dale Kyler, had lived in Ridgeway his whole life and never got so much as a speeding ticket.

The road turned from paved to gravel to just two tire tracks, running along the heavily wooded coastline of the lake. This was the quiet part of the lake, and distinctly different from the wealthy neighborhood of Lakeshore, even though it was only a few miles north. She had gotten Dale's favorite fishing location from Wanda Sims, his landlord, who seemed relieved that

Goodwin was taking Dale's disappearance seriously.

Goodwin slowed down and found the small gravel lot, imperceptible to those who did not know its location. Goodwin had assumed that the fishing spot would be a bust, that whatever happened to Dale and Jeff had happened on the trip there or back. But as Goodwin parked her charger, she realized she was wrong.

The old Bronco, the very same one that Jeff had driven to the station, sat in the gravel lot. The car's doors were thrown open and the keys were still in the ignition. Sunlight illuminated the spider silk and thin layer of dust that had already formed inside the vehicle.

Goodwin got out of her charger, calling out to see if anyone was around. All she heard was birdsong, and her own voice echoing off of the lake. Goodwin tried to have no emotional attachment in her cases. She needed a clear head to see all the facts as they unfolded. But she could not stop the dread that was creeping up her throat as she approached the Bronco. Her instincts told her that something was very wrong here.

Careful not to touch anything, Goodwin peered into the car. Inside she saw not one but two men's wallets. Donning gloves, she opened one wallet after the other. Jeffrey Wright's wallet held nothing but his ID and a few expired credit cards, but Dale's wallet contained a debit card and a little over a hundred dollars in cash.

Goodwin groaned. The *running off to a new town* theory was officially out. Dale and Jeff were most likely dead. Goodwin called in a tow for the Bronco, which would take a couple hours this far out. In the meantime she could search for more clues as to what happened here.

She searched the rest of the car and found nothing. Jim Weaver, Dale's boss, had told her that Dale carried a small gun in his car, but Goodwin did not find it. The empty glove box hung open like the mouth of a dead man.

Goodwin noticed a set of tracks in the mud, leading from the Bronco to the dock where some chairs and a cooler were set up. She snapped a few pictures for evidence before following the tracks up onto the dilapidated structure. The boards groaned as she walked carefully past two folding chairs with fishing poles bobbing in the water, the bait long gone. Inside the cooler a couple cans of beer floated in warm water. The scene looked as if someone had just stepped away and was intending to come back at any moment.

What had happened to Jeff after he had left the police station? What had happened to Dale? She tried to remember Jeff's crazy story, something about Dale being sucked into the lake.

They could have drowned, of course. It was not uncommon in a lakeside town, especially when alcohol was involved. But Goodwin found it hard to believe that two men who had grown up swimming in this lake would suddenly drown in it, especially so close to shore.

She stood on the dock, listening to the waves lap the shoreline. Despite the sweltering day and her love of swimming, Goodwin felt no urge to jump in. The water was strangely dark here, as if no sunbeams could penetrate the murky surface, only velvety blackness as far as the eye could see. When the wind caught the water Goodwin got a whiff of something evil, the smell of rotting flesh. A dead animal or something.

Or something.

A bright light glinted at the end of the dock, catching Goodwin's eye. She went to investigate and found a Smith & Wesson pistol, the exact kind that Dale supposedly kept in his glove box. Did Jeff, bereft over whatever happened to Dale, shoot himself and fall into the water? It was a promising theory, but one that was quickly dashed when Goodwin saw that all of the bullets were still in the gun's chamber.

She took a picture and tagged the gun for evidence, taking it back to her police cruiser. She wouldn't admit it to anyone else, but the dock gave her the creeps. Something about all that sludgy water below her. She felt a strong sense of menace coming from the water and was happy to be back on land.

After logging the evidence Goodwin got her extendable walking stick and started poking around the reeds near the shore. She didn't find anything other than a few empty beer cans that had blown off the dock, but she did notice a small deer path that led north along the lake's shore. She figured it was as good a place as any to continue her search.

She was surprised at how much cooler it was under the shade of the trees, and it took her eyes a moment to adjust to the light change. It was beautiful at this part of the lake, the woods dense with wild berry bushes, the air filled with birdsong. Beams of light reflected up onto the undersides of the trees closest to the lake, and they reminded Goodwin of fire.

Fire.

Suddenly, she was there again. The soot filling her nostrils, the sound of screaming and the rush of fire ringing in her ears as the flames grew all around her, licking up the side of her head and sealing her ear shut forever as she ran towards the cries of someone she could never save…

Goodwin shook her head, hard. She couldn't do this right now. Ideally she would do it never, but especially not right now. The nightmares were bad enough. She continued on the shoreline, poking and prodding any suspicious looking clumps of weeds or trash, hoping to find some kind of clue as to what happened to Dale and Jeff.

Goodwin supposed that other people liked walking in the woods, but it was never something she particularly enjoyed. She had spent most of her career in the city. The move to Ridgeway was supposed to be restorative for her– a beat cop in a sleepy little town where nothing happens. So much for that.

The woods here felt creepy. There was something about that dark lake, the whispering trees, the spongy leaves of the forest floor. This place didn't just have secrets, it was saturated in them. The trees towered over her in congress like unseeing judges– knowing the truth but unable, or unwilling, to help her. Goodwin could not shake the feeling that she was being watched by something in the water, something low, tracking her every move.

She spotted a bright flash, tangled in the roots and mud of the shoreline. Steadying herself against a large oak tree Goodwin reached into the mire and pulled out an old metal zippo lighter. She wiped it off to reveal a relief of an American eagle on one side, flag clutched in one proud claw. A name was engraved on the other side: DALE KYLER. Goodwin tagged the evidence and returned to the trail. She was just about to turn back when a thin, rusted voice rang out.

"Oh good, you found it."

Goodwin, a hardened police officer, nearly screamed. The voice had not come from behind or in front of her, but rather above her. Down from the tree canopy like the last drops of rain. Goodwin, her hand on her gun, demanded that whoever was there show themselves.

There was a pause so long that Goodwin was starting to wonder if she had imagined the voice. She looked down the path she had walked and found that she had gone a lot further into the forest than she thought—she could no longer see the parking lot, only a wall of green behind her.

When she turned back to the lake, a woman stood before her.

She was very small and hunched, with thick ropy arms. She had black dreadlocks full of beads and bird skulls, tied back from her filthy, smiling face. She was wearing layers and layers of rags, and smelled of campfire and dirt. She had Asian features, but it was impossible to tell her age. Her face was strangely smooth, and upon closer inspection, Goodwin saw small symbols tattooed under her eyes. So this must be the "witch of the lake" that she had heard about.

The woman surveyed Goodwin with shiny black eyes, like a curious crow. "Are you going to shoot me with that gun?" The woman nodded to Goodwin's hand, which still rested on the butt of her weapon.

"No." Goodwin showed the woman her open palms. "I mean you no harm. I'm looking for some people who went missing."

"I know," the woman replied. In the shifting light she seemed to blend into the forest, as if disappearing before Goodwin's eyes. She smiled like a cat, with several blackened and missing teeth. Her long eye teeth had been plated with silver. Goodwin had worked with a lot of homeless people but had never seen gold and silver teeth outside of a pirate movie. The woman appeared harmless but was undeniably creepy. Goodwin had not said this out loud, but the woman's smile dropped anyway.

"Like you're so pretty to look at," she snarled.

Goodwin stared at her, mouth agape.

The woman continued. "I am Psyche. And you are correct, I am the witch of the lake." Goodwin realized Psyche had moved closer to her without her noticing. Now she was less than two feet away, staring hard at Goodwin. Goodwin fought to keep her cool as the woman looked quizzically at her scar.

"How did you burn your face?" Psyche reached out a filthy finger to stroke Goodwin's ruined ear.

"A fire." Goodwin stepped away in a smooth motion. Psyche seemed to find this deliciously funny. She threw her head back, laughing heartily. It sounded like something between a raven's caw and a smoker's cough.

"Oh you are a bright one. " Psyche wiped tears from her eyes. Goodwin shook herself, trying to stay on task. If anyone knew what happened here, it was probably this woman.

"And you are right again," said Psyche. "I do know what is happening here. But I can't tell you."

This time the woman's voice had come from behind Goodwin, right into her good ear. Goodwin whirled around to see that Psyche was less than a foot behind her, close enough to smell her pungently. Goodwin jerked away from Psyche's leering face, but she did not reach for her gun.

Whatever this woman was, Goodwin's gut told her that Psyche was not a threat to her. Cop's instincts. She swallowed and asked, "What do you know? Why can't you tell me?"

Psyche looked Goodwin up and down, apparently deciding whether Goodwin was worth trusting. Goodwin matched her gaze with her own. When Psyche finally spoke, it was in a conspiratorial whisper, turned away from the lake, as though it was listening.

"The girl that went missing. The one that was with child…"

"Amber Prenley?" Goodwin asked hopefully, pulling a folded missing poster from her pocket.

Psyche nodded slowly. "Officer, this lake…it is a special place. A fertile place. A seed has been planted in the lake. The thing about seeds is that they can grow anywhere that is fertile. Seeds don't care if they were tended in a garden or if they were shit out by a bird, as long as they land somewhere they can grow. You get it?"

"No," answered Goodwin flatly. She had hoped that Psyche could help her, but now she was just babbling nonsense. Goodwin figured it was meth, which would explain the teeth…

Psyche shot Goodwin a sneer, and once again Goodwin was convinced she knew her thoughts.

"I can't tell you if you don't want to know," the woman growled. "Seeds bloom into truth, Officer Goodwin. They bloom into knowledge. They bloom into other things too. All different sorts of dark things can grow in that lake."

"Wait, how did you know my na–"

Psyche shushed her. She cocked her head, listening. Goodwin had noticed that the forest had become strangely quiet. No rustling of leaves, the birds had paused their song and now all she could hear was the lapping of the lake.

When Psyche spoke again it was in low furtive tones. "I could tell you the truth, but you won't believe it and I do not like to waste my time," hissed Psyche. "But I will leave you with this: more people are going to die when this seed blooms. You need to know 'what is happening here.'"

To Goodwin's horror, Psyche reached inside of her own mouth. There was a crunching sound, and Psyche's fingers reappeared– slick with blood. In her dirty palm she held a tooth. The tooth was long and pointed– Goodwin would not have believed it came from a human if she hadn't just seen Psyche pull it from her own head.

Psyche snapped a few leaves off of nearby trees and deftly wrapped the tooth in a neat package of green. She dropped the package on the ground between them, stepping back into the forest.

"If you want to know what happened to that poor girl and her baby, Officer Goodwin, swallow that tooth."

A loud sound broke the silence. It was the tow truck Goodwin called, rattling into the lot for the Bronco. Its clanking engine sounded deafening in the forest. Numbly, Goodwin realized she was in the woods just outside the parking lot. But that was not possible– she knew she had walked at least a mile down the coast. She could just barely see the spot where she had gotten the lighter in between the trees. How did she get back here?

Goodwin turned back and Psyche was gone. She stood alone, listening to the lapping of waves. Her radio chirped, announcing the tow truck's presence.

On the ground before her lay the leaf bundle containing Psyche's tooth. Before she could second guess herself, Goodwin grabbed it. She slipped the bundle into her pocket and headed back to the parking lot to deal with the tow.

CHAPTER TEN

RIDGEWAY HAD BEEN PLENTY CONCERNED about Amber Prenley. Anyone who spoke to Gloria Prenley knew that her daughter did not, could not, leave of her own accord. Her MISSING poster still hung on every lamp post in town, faded by the sun.

But as weeks wore on, Gloria left the house less and less, and soon new theories began to arise. Ridgeway was an old-fashioned town, and Amber had been unmarried and pregnant. Many people wondered if Amber had been "sent away" to have the baby, others agreed with Breeson's theory that she had taken off with the child's father. Slowly the community had begun to move on.

That was until word of Dale Kyler and Jeff Wright's disappearance hit the gossip mill. One person missing could be a fluke, but three presented a real danger. Ridgeway was a small and tight-knit community. People had accidents, they got hurt, they even died. But they didn't vanish into thin air.

Like herd animals, the people of Ridgeway began a panicked circle looking for predators within the group. After news of the abandoned Bronco and gun got out, the locals put even more pressure on Breeson to find out what was going on.

The Sheriff had to admit that it was unlikely that Dale and Jeff would have left town without their only means of transportation, or Dale's beloved lighter. Apparently it was a gift from his late wife, and Dale never went anywhere without it.

Sheriff Breeson arranged for a Search and Rescue team from the neighboring township to come over to search the forest and shoreline where the Bronco had been found. They would be there this Friday, and boats with radar from the state would be able to search the water the Friday after.

Goodwin was glad that Breeson had finally gotten off his ass, but as far as she was concerned it was too little, too late. She knew that Breeson's close ties with Grant Wellworth, or more accurately Grant Wellworth's donations, meant that no one would be able to interview Hunter.

Goodwin also knew that Hunter had something to do with Amber's disappearance, but she had to admit that the disappearance of Jeff and Dale was baffling. After all, she was the last person to see Jeff Wright alive. Could Hunter also have been involved in the murder of these two men? Some kind of cover-up? Or are they dealing with two completely separate incidents? Maybe the panicked townspeople were right, and a serial killer was on the loose. Some random drifter killer. But how would they lure Amber from her home?

Goodwin sat on her back deck, mulling over the facts and watching fireflies dance in the suffocating night. She cracked open another beer, her bare feet on the railing of her porch. She had rented a three-bed, two-bath house surrounded by woodland for a fraction of what she paid for her apartment in the city. An upside of living in a place no one else wanted to. Goodwin slapped mosquitos off her legs and drank beer. Next to her sat a neat row of empty bottles. She used to love going out to drink at bars. It was an easy way to meet people and socialize on a rare night off.

After the fire she couldn't handle the stares. So now she drank alone.

Goodwin thought about the woman she had met in the forest, Psyche. The so-called "witch of the lake." Goodwin hadn't told anyone about her. If Breeson didn't want to listen when she had real evidence, she doubted he would care about the ramblings of the local homeless woman.

Still, she had kept the tooth.

Goodwin went inside. It was dark outside, but Goodwin often kept the lights off in her home. Another thing that she had started doing after she was burned. She got another beer from the fridge and threw a TV dinner in the microwave.

The house was quiet. The solitude might be uncomfortable to others, but Goodwin preferred it. Unseen and unseeable on her own turf, a creature within its den.

On the kitchen counter, lit by the whirring microwave, lay the little leaf package containing Psyche's tooth. Intellectually, Goodwin knew that the whole thing was insane. She had seen a lot of things in her time– some explainable, some not. But she could not stop thinking about how Psyche appeared to have read her thoughts, how she seemed to jump from place to place without moving. Whatever was going on with these disappearances was weird. Could going a weird route be the way to solve it?

Goodwin knew that cops don't investigate by swallowing random body parts handed to them by indigents. And yet she found herself considering it. Not just considering it, but seriously considering it. All she could think about were those photos of Amber Prenley at her mother's house, those pool blue eyes. Amber Prenley had not run away, and not knowing what happened to her was eating Goodwin alive. Goodwin wanted to find her, to save her. Even if she was beyond saving, Goodwin wanted to bring Amber and her unborn baby home.

Goodwin made a choice. She steeled herself, ripped open the leaf package and retrieved the tooth.

It smelled of morning breath, smoke, and lake mud. Before Goodwin could think better of it, she threw the tooth in her mouth and washed it down with a big swig of beer.

Goodwin felt the tooth scrape, claw-like, down the inside of her throat. The effect was immediate. She collapsed onto the linoleum of her kitchen, the beer foamed up out of her mouth like a snake, purging her. She fell to the floor and kept falling, falling down, down into complete blackness. A dirty, wet blackness.

For a moment, Goodwin swirled in the nothingness, her body unresponsive as her mind screamed in panic. Then all was quiet. The darkness parted, and Goodwin could see clear water. Not like the dirty water she had seen at the end of the dock; this was bright freshwater shimmering under the moonlight. The moon looked strange, it wavered, and it took her a moment to realize that she was underwater, at least half a mile below the surface. The moon glinted at her through the water like a distant eye.

A strange dread filled the lake, a disturbance across the surface. Goodwin heard an engine, then saw a small fishing boat slip towards them like a water snake. The engine purred quietly, the sound of an expensive and well-working machine. Once it was overhead the driver of the boat killed the engine, and all was quiet.

There was a loud thump. And then another. The boat rocked unsteadily, side to side, as if someone on the craft was struggling to move something heavy. A blue mass hung over the side of the boat just above the water.

There was a loud splash. Goodwin could see a blue tarp, wrapped around something bulky that was weighed down with iron chains and cement blocks. Once the figure had been thrown into the lake and began its descent towards Goodwin, the boat engine kicked back to life. The small craft whisked away as quickly and quietly as it had come.

Goodwin watched the figure descend, silhouetted in the moonlight. Down, down, down came the blue tarp, its corners flapping, its chains yanking it to the lake's floor. It came to settle before her, and with horror Goodwin saw what it was.

The tarp was wrapped around a human body, one with the obvious distended midsection of pregnancy. From one end of the plastic burial shroud floated a few strands of auburn hair. From the other stuck a pair of small white feet, still wearing a single green croc.

There was a pulse in the lake. A transfer of energy, physical as an electric shock. Another, faster now, and something underneath the tarp began to twist. It was as if a live animal had been trapped in the folds and was thrashing wildly for freedom. The chains bobbed ominously as the corpse began to writhe. The pregnant midsection started to swell as another sound surrounded them, a low thrumming. To Goodwin, it almost sounded like a deep, sinister laugh. The body twitched and convulsed. An inhuman voice was rising from the lake floor. Words in ancient languages slipped by Goodwin like fish. She was terrified but could not scream.

The body in the tarp stopped twitching, An invisible knife carved a slit in the tarp over the abdomen, revealing blueish, distended flesh. From there the skin of Amber's pregnant stomach began to split open. Blood ballooned out of the fresh corpse, and soon the surrounding water filled with bright crimson swirls, obscuring the body and its eldritch transformation.

Blood filled Goodwin's vision like silk in the moonlight. As it turned in the water the blood went from crimson to black. It settled to reveal the opened body, still wrapped in a tarp and chained to the lakebed. From the vivisected abdomen poured a corrupt, rotted blackness as thick as oil. It spilled out, moving along the lake floor, covering seaweed and blotting out all light.

A baby's cry cut through the water, bright and undistorted. The human sound was at odds with the horror before her as long, slick tendrils appeared from the blackness. Soon they were all around, corrupting the water and sliding over each other like a mass of eels. But this was no natural creature. What blossomed before Goodwin was something wrong, something obscene, a perversion of nature.

The tendrils reached up from the body, they swirled together like a huge sea anemone, searching for something. As Goodwin watched the creature put forth a long stalk, with a bulging end like the bud of a lotus flower.

The bud bloomed, and in the center was the head of a deceased human baby. Slowly, the head turned to face Goodwin. In a shaft of moonlight she could see the blue veins in the baby's delicate eyelids, the soft curve of its ears. And then the eyelids fluttered open, and from the empty sockets oozed filthy lake mud.

The tendrils reached towards Goodwin, and she could feel their death cold, slick with decay. The blackness again settled over her.

She awoke with a scream.

She was back in her house, in the dark dining room, face down in a puddle of her own vomit. As she gathered her bearings, wiping the congealed mess away from her face, she saw the tooth Psyche had given her. It glittered in the sick. All Goodwin could think about was the monstrosity that had crawled out of Amber's dead body. Psyche's words hung in her head,

"More people are going to die when this seed blooms. "

CHAPTER ELEVEN

HUNTER WELLWORTH COULDN'T SLEEP.

He sat out on the porch of his lake house, nursing a whiskey on ice and staring out over the lake, the reflection of the water leaving ghostly ripples on his face. His wife, Tabby, slept in a medicated dream, and both of the boys had gone to bed hours ago.

For the first time in Hunter's life, the lake looked foreign to him. The Wellworths had lived by Lake Munahegan for nearly a century, and the lake was as much a part of Hunter's legacy as the bank and the property on the shore. All for him to enjoy and pass down to Tanner when the time came.

But the lake had changed, darkening like a bruise under the eye of an opponent. He felt hostility coming off of the water with every lap on the shore.

Hunter did not like these new changes going on. He had been confident that the interest in Amber's disappearance had begun to die down. People had stopped talking about her around town, and Hunter had discreetly taken her missing posters down at the bank. It looked like everything was going to go back to normal. Then those two idiot rednecks went missing, and the whole thing got kicked up again.

Hunter swirled his glass. He didn't like that burned bitch sniffing around. Sheriff Breeson had assured Hunter and his father that Officer Goodwin had been reprimanded and removed from the case. Hunter had wanted her fired, but Breeson said he couldn't afford to lose her.

Hunter decided that Officer Goodwin knew too much, and she had the damn ring. It was hardly slam dunk evidence, but it certainly didn't make him look good.

He took a long sip of his whiskey. Wind began to rise off of the water, bringing with it a wet, rotten smell. Hunter knew that giving Amber the ring had been stupid, but promising to marry her was the only thing that shut her up. When Amber got pregnant she had shown up at the house like a bat out of hell, insisting that the baby was his. Hunter didn't believe her, and he had considered his offer of abortion money generous.

But Amber was having none of it. She said that if Hunter didn't divorce Tabby and marry her, she was going to get a paternity test and take him to court for child support. But first, she would tell everyone she knew who the baby's father was. So Hunter had given her the ring to buy some time.

Hunter shook his head. It was her own fault, backing him into a corner like that. Hunter was the first-born son, the heir to the Wellworth dynasty. He had a name to protect, a legacy to pass down to Tanner.

If word got out that he had knocked up the teenage babysitter, his name would be ruined. He had a family to think of, a real family. And here was Amber flaunting her pregnant belly around, making everyone ask questions. He had to do something, and he had to do it before the little bastard was born.

The air was hot and soupy in his lungs. He knocked back the last drops of whiskey and turned to enter the house, feeling he might as well try to get a few hours of sleep before work tomorrow.

The door behind him was open.

Hunter never left doors open. He knew that he had closed this door behind him. As he got closer, he saw footprints trailing into the house. Small, muddy footprints. Too small to be a man, but larger than either of his sons. A woman's footprint, in black lake mud.

He looked around the darkened living room, the expensive white furniture like hulking statues in the moonlight. There was no one there.

Hunter tried to tell himself that the footprints had been there before he stepped out on the deck. Gloria Prenley was on indefinite hiatus from her cleaning duties, and the substitute cleaners did a shit job. Maybe he was so distracted that he did not see the footprints until now.

But the footprints were fresh mud, not dried. With his heart hammering in his chest Hunter followed the prints past the kitchen, and up the crafted wooden stairs. The footprints led down the hallway, past the master where his wife lay sleeping, and to the door of Tanner's bedroom.

Tanner, terrified of the dark, always kept his door ajar. As Hunter approached, he heard a strange noise coming from his son's bedroom. A wet, slushy sound that reminded Hunter of gutted fish. It made his skin crawl. The hallway was filled with the smell of earth, rot, and lake water. Hunter pushed open the door and screamed.

A figure was standing over Tanner's bed, leaning over his sleeping face. The thing had impossibly long arms. It appeared to be covered in massive black worms that slithered over each other in the near dark, dripping mud and oozing all over the carpet. When Hunter opened the door, the creature turned to look at him.

Hunter saw the rotten, bloated, and unmistakable face of Amber Prenley.

Hunter turned on the light and she was gone. Well, not completely. The window to Tanner's second story bedroom was open, and in the first few seconds of artificial yellow light Hunter saw something black and slimy slip out of the window.

Tanner, hair mussed from sleep and wearing only stained whitey-tighties, sat up in bed and began to cry, wailing for his mother. Hunter ignored his son, running to the open window and looking out onto the lawn, the dock, and the lake.

There was nothing. Nothing but small ripples at the end of the dock, barely visible at this distance.

Hunter looked back into the hallway, now illuminated by the bedroom light. The footprints were gone. He heaved a sigh of relief. He must have been dreaming, the whiskey and his dark thoughts making him paranoid. He tried to get a hold of himself while his eldest son stared at him, eyes wide with terror.

"Daddy! What is it?" screamed Tanner, lunging out of bed. Hunter was not worried about waking up Tabby, who slept with enough sedatives to kill a horse. But he was suddenly embarrassed by his overreaction.

Hunter grabbed his son and, not interested in playing the good father, gruffly shoved the boy back into bed.

"Stay with me until I fall asleep!" howled Tanner. Hunter gritted his teeth but agreed, though he insisted on turning out the light.

"Why did you scream?" asked Tanner after he had settled back down into bed.

"I didn't. Go to sleep." Hunter was over his fright and began to feel like his son was making a production number of this whole thing. But he stayed put– feeling vaguely bad about jolting the boy awake. Finally the sound of Tanner's soft snoring resumed and Hunter walked over to look at his firstborn boy.

Hunter did not like parenting. He did not enjoy either of his sons, but he felt a strong blood-spattered love for his eldest. In Tanner he saw the future of his family.

Tanner's face was swollen and red, eyelashes matted with tears like a baby. Hunter sneered—Tanner was too old to cry. Tabby had always babied him. He was going to need to be a real man to take on the Wellworth legacy. Hunter decided that he would sign Tanner up for football to toughen him up.

In this new calm Hunter had forgotten about his earlier fright, the transition softened by all the whisky. Hunter crept out, shutting the door to his son's room behind him. As he turned down the darkened hallway to the master bedroom, he nearly screamed again.

A figure was standing in the dark of the hallway, just outside of Hunter's reach. A dark silhouette, still and staring.

It took Hunter several panicked moments to realize that the figure was his other son, Jay. Hunter gritted his teeth. He had always detested Jay, who he privately believed to be weak, effeminate, and useless. Hunter was in no mood for Jay's weird bullshit, not tonight.

"Jay! What are you doing out of bed?"

"Talking to Amber," whispered Jay. In the dark, Hunter could only see Jay's outline. He couldn't see the boy's mouth move. Just a whispered voice that seemed to come from all around him.

"Stop being stupid," snapped Hunter. "Get back in bed before I belt you."

"Amber told me to tell you something."

"Goddammit Jay, I am going to count to three, and if you are not in bed by the time I—"

"She said you completed the ritual, and now she is coming back. She said to tell you that she is going to take something precious from you, just like you took something precious from her. "

Hunter, furious and terrified, cocked his arm back to smack Jay. But when he struck, his palm swung through empty air, cracking into the wall opposite. Jay was gone, his door closed. Hunter stood alone in the hallway, holding his injured hand. A cold draft whisked through the house from the still-open deck door, making a sound like a giggle.

CHAPTER TWELVE

OFFICER GOODWIN AWOKE THE MORNING after her vision with a terrible headache and a bad taste in her mouth. She decided that the whole incident with the tooth had been a fever dream. She was just working too hard on the case, spending too much time thinking about what could have happened to Amber. That, combined with some kind of food poisoning, caused vomiting and terrible dreams.

She felt like she had a hangover. It was enough to ruin anyone's morning. When she caught sight of herself in the mirror she saw that her face was gray. The scarred part of her neck and ear tingled, as if remembering its insult. She tried to dismiss the dream, but the images of Amber's body bursting open to reveal that terrible dark creature flashed before her like pop-up ads from hell.

She took a cold shower and tried to clear her head. Goodwin had work to do. Today was the first day of the volunteer search of Lake Munahegan's upper shore. Sheriff Breeson had delegated Goodwin to supervise a small group of volunteers. Together they would search the two miles north of the dock while Breeson and the search team from the county would check the area where Goodwin found Dale's lighter.

Normally, Goodwin would be annoyed by this slight. She was the one who found the lighter, and that was despite Breeson, not because of him. Yet she found she was relieved to not have to go back to that part of the forest. She didn't want to see Psyche again.

Goodwin drove to a convenience store for a coffee and a neon blue sports drink. Her volunteers would be meeting at a different gravel lot than the one where the abandoned Bronco was found. It was farther north, more easily accessible from the main road that cut through town. This gravel lot stood right next to a trailhead that locals used for hiking and featured a few lakeside BBQs for public use.

When Goodwin arrived, it was early and already hot. She cruised into the parking lot and saw that most of the volunteers were already there.

Several Ridgeway locals waited for Goodwin in a copse of tall fir trees by the lakeshore. There was Mrs. Edith Wrangler, the owner of the Wrangler Diner. She was an older version of her daughter Sherry, with thick gray hair swept into a bun. There was also Harold Spell from the hardware store. A spotty teenager, Brendan Sims, had been sent by his mother, Wanda Sims, who was Dale's landlady. Jim Weaver, Dale's boss at the gas station, had also volunteered. When Goodwin saw Jim he looked relieved, as if glad to be doing something to help find Dale.

Gloria Prenley was also in the search parties, but she was with Sheriff Breeson's group. Goodwin wanted to believe that meant that Breeson was taking Amber's case seriously. The cynical side of her thought that it was more likely that Sheriff Breeson wanted to get a picture with Gloria for the local press.

As Goodwin walked up to the volunteer group she saw Jim Weaver talking to Harold and Edith, shaking his head slowly. Goodwin caught snippets of their conversation on the lake breeze–

"He's been fishing that spot for the past thirty years, and then one night he just vanishes? It doesn't make any sense. I am telling you, there's something in that lake…"

"What do you mean?" interrupted Goodwin. "What does the lake have to do with this?"

She startled Jim Weaver, who looked at her and then quickly looked away. The rest followed suit.

They stood in awkward silence until finally, Edith Wrangler spoke. "The water has gone dark, see?" She gestured to the lake that lay beyond the trees.

"And?" asked Goodwin.

"Well, some people 'round here think it's a bad omen." Edith chuckled self-consciously. "Just old-fashioned superstition."

"And it smells like shit," grumbled Brendan, who didn't look up from his cellphone. Goodwin had to agree. The area was beautiful, all dappled sunlight and old-growth pine forest. But there was a fetid smell coming off of the water, mixing with the hot summer air. When Goodwin peered through the trees she could see that the water was dark, almost matte in the brilliant sunlight.

"Did you alert the environmental agencies?" asked Goodwin, stumbling because she didn't know what the local water testing organization was called.

"Yup." answered Harold Spell after spitting out a wad of tobacco. "They won't even come down and look. Said it was a 'bacterial overgrowth' and not worth their time as long as it doesn't spread to the water supply. Ridgeway gets their water from upstream."

"I see," said Goodwin. But she was gone from that place, back in the waters of her dream. All the filth spilling out of Amber's body, tainting the water all around it, making the clear water thick and wretched....

Goodwin realized that everyone was looking at her. She cleared her throat and focused on the task at hand.

"For those I have not met yet, I'm Officer Goodwin. I know you're all upset by Amber, Dale, and Jeff's disappearances. I am too. So let's get to work searching, and hopefully we can get to the bottom of this. We will form a line and move through this area inch by inch."

Goodwin and the townsfolk got to work poking and prodding the forest floor beside the lake. The hot sun hit patches of needles through the trees, aromatic pine wafting on the breeze from the water, making the smell more bearable. The forest was in full glory. Red berries covered pricker bushes and clumps of mushrooms popped out of fallen logs. Birds tittered in the canopy. If they weren't searching for dead bodies, it would be an almost pleasant way to spend the afternoon.

They took a break for lunch, which had been brought in gratis from the Wrangler Diner. No one spoke while they worked. The sun made its way across the sky, and before Goodwin knew it the designated area had been thoroughly covered. Aside from a few beer cans and old tires, they had found nothing. But Goodwin had been impressed by how hard the townsfolk looked for one of their own. Even the mulish Brandon had scrambled down the wash outs and poked around fox holes to look for clues. Coming from the anonymity of the big city, the coziness of the community was touching. These people cared; they were worried.

They were right to be worried.

Goodwin sat in her cruiser after everyone had left. Breeson had told her via the radio that they hadn't found anything in their search either, though they hoped to have more luck when the boat team came in. He had been more cooperative as of late and less snappy. Goodwin thought it was just a show for the state cops who had muscled into the Ridgeway department. She appreciated it all the same.

Goodwin didn't know what she was waiting for. As the sun cast glorious magenta and orange hues across the sky she thought about not just Amber, but Dale and Jeff.

"What happened to you guys?" Goodwin muttered, staring out at the lake. Goodwin remembered the panic in Jeff Wright's voice when he told her about something in the lake reaching up and pulling his cousin under. He said that it was black and slick—

"Storm's coming," came a voice from beside her.

Goodwin screamed. The passenger seat of her cruiser, which had been locked and empty, now contained the grinning form of Psyche. Goodwin stared at her, mouth agape. The windows were down, but Goodwin had no idea how she could have crawled into the car without her noticing. Psyche smiled like a cat, her silver-plated teeth flashing.

"Did you swallow the tooth?"

Goodwin just glared at her.

"I suppose that's a yes." Psyche chuckled. "I can see it in your eyes. You look drained."

"I can't hear you," grumbled Goodwin. "You're talking into my bad ear."

Goodwin was struck by the expression on Psyche's strange, ageless face. She looked embarrassed, genuinely sorry for the faux paus. She reached out as if to touch Goodwin's shoulder. Goodwin glared and Psyche thought better of it.

"My apologies." Psyche was now standing next to Goodwin's driver's side window, leaning down slightly to look her in the eye. Goodwin winced. How did she move like that? Did she flip over the car, like an acrobat? She steadied her breath before saying:

"It's alright. Lots of people forget I'm deaf on that side. Just please stay put while we are talking."

"Sure thing. So now that you've swallowed the tooth, do you understand what is going on here? What happened to poor Amber Prenley?"

Goodwin decided to play along. "Sure. But I still need to find their bodies before we can–"

Psyche shook her head. "No. No bodies. They have been absorbed. And it's too late to save the next one."

"What?" Goodwin responded. "The next one? How do you know it will happen again? What is happening to these people, Psyche? If you know, you need to tell me."

Psyche began to look uncomfortable. She shifted her weight from foot to foot, which were wrapped in several layers of old rags. She glanced nervously over her shoulder to the lake, the beads in her dreadlocks clanking like reeds.

"The beast chooses its victims to spite its creator. Once it has discovered what will hurt its creator the most, it uses it as bait."

"That makes no sense and doesn't help me at all." Goodwin snapped. Psyche grinned, holding up her hands. Goodwin noted with horror that Psyche had no fingernails— her long digits tapered into uniform black points, like a stick that was used to turn a fire.

"I can't talk to you here. Storm's coming."

"You keep saying that, but there isn't a cloud in the sky," grumbled Goodwin. She was exhausted and filthy from spending all day digging through the woods. She was starting to believe that Psyche was messing with her.

"Come to the old dock at midnight tonight. I will show you the creature. You can see it take its victim with your own two eyes."

Goodwin perked up.

But Psyche shook her head. "You won't be able to stop it. The path is predestined. Come at midnight, you will see."

"I'm a police officer, and if you know of a crime that's about to take place, you need to tell me." Goodwin reached for her notebook. It took her a few seconds to realize that she was speaking to air.

She sat alone in the steaming hot parking lot, staring at the woods and the lake. The sunset continued to throw fantastic shades across the sky. But along the distant tree line, barely visible, Goodwin could make out dark storm clouds.

CHAPTER THIRTEEN

"I WANT TO TAKE MY boat out on the lake!" screamed Tanner. He was standing at the edge of the living room, glaring at his parents. His face flamed with indignation. He was wearing a full boating outfit, complete with his boating shoes. He looked like an exact miniature of his father. Hunter was staring out of the large window with his back to his son, ignoring him.

Tanner had been hounding his mother about going out on his boat for over an hour. But the weather had turned nasty. Even with a floodlight, the lake was too dark. Heavy clouds loomed over the lake's slick black surface. The moody blues and purples colored the inside of the lake house. Hunter was in a brooding mood and had kept all the lights off, giving the living room a ghostly feel.

"It's going to rain soon, and it's almost dark, honey…." cajoled Tabby, slurring her words slightly. She had spent the better part of the day on a wine-tasting tour with her friends. She missed Amber, who always kept the boys occupied and out of her hair. She wished that it was Jay sitting with them and not her obnoxious oldest. Jay never gave her any trouble. But she hadn't seen Jay since the morning. It was as if he was hiding.

Tanner continued wailing about the boat. Sunburnt and drunk, Tabby turned plaintively towards her husband to help her. He continued to ignore both of them, facing the glowering lake and drinking a large gin and tonic with clinking ice.

"Why is it so important to go now?" sighed Tabby., "Can't you just wait until tom–"

"Daddy!" squealed Tanner. "Tell her I can take the boat out!"

Hunter swung around.

"Shut up," he hissed venomously "Are you an idiot? Can't you see it's about to storm? Go to your room, you irritating shit."

Tabby and Tanner were shocked. Hunter was usually terse, but he was never so nasty, especially not with his oldest.

Tanner hiccupped and then burst into tears, running from the room. He turned on the light in the hallway as he mounted the stairs.

"TURN THAT FUCKING LIGHT OFF," screamed Hunter. Tanner did as he was told, and scurried up the stairs, whimpering.

Hunter returned to his drink and the lake, radiating stony anger.

"You didn't have to come down so hard on him," whispered Tabby.

"Oh so *now* you're a parent?" snarled Hunter, "You've been running around all day getting drunk with your friends, spending my money. Leaving me with these fucking kids. Some mother you are. You can fuck off too."

Tabby sat, stunned. Hunter slammed down his drink on a table, hard enough to crack the glass. He turned on his heel, walked over to his wife, and wrenched her to her feet. Tabitha gave a startled yelp as her husband half-shoved, half-threw her toward the staircase.

"Go sober up!" he shouted. Tabitha gave him one last look, her eyes wide with fear and hurt, before she scurried away.

Hunter threw himself down on the couch. Being the man of the house was like jogging through quicksand. The harder he struggled, the more it all weighed him down. Tabitha and the boys were a millstone around his neck. They had no appreciation of what he did for them, the things he had done to protect their family…

The rain started to fall, pattering against the tall glass windows. It was like a thousand knocks to be let inside, a thousand pleas, a thousand demands. Hunter sat back on the couch and covered his eyes with his hands.

He fell asleep.

He awoke hours later, hearing the storm battering the lake house.

There was a flash of lightning, and Hunter saw Jay standing before him. Just as he had the other night, Jay was silhouetted against the window, a dark figure framed by the storm. Thunder rumbled in the distance and the rain thrashed against the window as father and son stared at each other in silence.

A voice filled the room, but Jay's mouth did not move.

"Something precious."

It was not Jay's voice. It was Amber Prenley's.

CHAPTER FOURTEEN

AT FIRST, OFFICER GOODWIN WAS grateful for the night's stormy weather. The rain brought relief from the miserable heat. But as she drove out to Dale Kyler's fishing spot she began to regret her decision to try to meet Psyche. It was too dark this far out in the country, and the rain made her headlights nearly useless. The downpour slashed against her cruiser, as she bounced over potholes, her headlights two slices of yellow rain. For all Goodwin knew, she could be driving directly into the lake.

Goodwin found the lot with some difficulty and parked the cruiser near the forest. She wrapped herself up in her rain gear. Rain pelted the car, and for a moment she considered turning around, having a drink, and going back to bed. She entertained the wonderful thought of pulling the covers up around her as the rain pattered on the roof.

But then another vision filled her mind. She saw the creature on the bottom of the lake, the black, foul tendrils slipping over each other. The horrible stalk and the baby's head, rising in front of her, its eyes made of mud...

Goodwin shuddered and got out of the car. In the lot she felt exposed. The surface of the lake writhed under the rain and wind, whipping up the foul smell of decay. In the distance, thunder growled like a great beast on the hunt. She didn't know where Psyche was or how she would find her. She didn't even know what they were looking for.

Goodwin trusted her instincts. Psyche was crazy and possibly had drugged her, but she still knew something. Goodwin gritted her teeth—if this was what she had to do to find Amber, so be it. Gloria Prenley had stopped calling the station and stopped hanging flyers around town. Rumor had it that she was holed up at home, withering away. She weighed heavily on Officer Goodwin's mind.

Goodwin walked into the forest, under the cover of the trees. It was like stepping into another world. It was dark in the forest, the kind of darkness that shifts and moves before your helpless eyes.

Anything could be in that forest.

The rain was less violent under the canopy of trees. Goodwin's eyes adjusted somewhat. She listened to the percussion of rain on leaves, the lake thrashing against the wooded shore. Goodwin felt a great tension here, the sound of silence after a scream. She also had the strong sensation of being watched.

Goodwin turned on her flashlight, swinging it through the dripping forest. She was on the deer path where she had found Dale's lighter. She passed the thin beam of light over the path in front of her and into the bramble on her left. When she swung it back, she jumped.

Before her was the skeletal form of Amber Prenley.

Her eyes, white and filled with green rot, bulged from her sockets. She was somehow both dried and wet as if her body had been mummified in mud. Her mouth hung open in a long, silent scream, fuzzy black tongue lolling over exposed jaw. She was wrapped in a blue tarp, but her abdomen was flayed open and hollow inside. Goodwin could see into the girl's exposed ribcage. From the wound poured an inky blackness, a horrible putrid blackness.

Goodwin jolted, dropping her flashlight. It rolled away behind her, and she scrambled to find it. When she got ahold of it she swung the flashlight back to the path. No one was there.

"Help me."

A voice whispered in the wind. It was soft, a girl's voice. Not a woman, but someone young, lost, and afraid.

"Please, please find us." Another voice, now a man, much older, and a smoker. The voice was tired and miserable.

"Please find my body." A different voice, also a man and heavy with a twangy accent, came from behind her.

"I don't want to be left here, I want to be buried by my mama... please..."

On the wind was the smell of the rotting lake, rolling under the rainfall. Thunder boomed across the sky, causing Goodwin to flinch. The hair on the back of her neck stood up as Goodwin flashed her light around.

"Psyche?" she whispered. She was met with silence, only the drip of rain on leaves. There was another flash of lightning, and in its illumination, Goodwin saw Psyche, high up in a tree. Psyche was staring down at her with a strange expression. It took a while for Goodwin to realize it was fear.

A roll of thunder shook the ground, and Goodwin flinched again. When she flashed her light at the tree where Psyche was, no one was there. Goodwin steeled herself, trying to swallow the hard lump of fear in her throat. She was a cop; it was just a storm; she needed to get a grip.

Goodwin walked towards the tree where Psyche had been.

Psyche's husky voice slipped past her shoulder, whispering into her good ear. "Follow me, and no matter what you see or hear, don't go off of the path."

Goodwin looked down. A clear path, one that had not been there before, split through the trees and undergrowth. The foliage moving made a sound, like retching earth. Though it was dark, Goodwin could clearly define the boundaries, the thick briar leaning away from the path as if pushed down by invisible hands.

Shaking, Goodwin pointed the flashlight down the path. The circle of yellow light trembled in the dark.

"Put that out!" Psyche snapped. "It'll see you!"

Goodwin did as she was told. A sense of menace moved all around them as palpable as the rain. Goodwin waited until her eyes adjusted to the darkness around her, then began to take careful steps along the path. She couldn't see Psyche but knew that she was behind her, nearby. Goodwin could smell her heavy scent of fire and dirt, strangely comforting in the storm. Her heart pounded in her chest.

A pale, glowing face appeared before her, hanging in her path. Goodwin stumbled back, mouth open. It was a child's face, one that she recognized, even though she had never seen the child alive.

"Why couldn't you save me?" the vision demanded. Its empty eyes oozed lake mud.

"Don't look," hissed Psyche. "Don't stop."

"You let me burn in the fire…"

Goodwin felt Psyche push her. She stumbled forward, looking down at her rain boots. The face and voice faded.

"Help us…" whispered the girl's voice again. "My baby…"

Goodwin focused on her feet and tried to ignore it.

Something grabbed her wrist. She turned to see that her arm had been hooked by the rotting form of a man. His legs had been torn away, and what was left of his maggot-ridden torso was bloated and unrecognizable. The ruined face looked up at Goodwin, eyes masses of water worms, its mouth full of lake mud.

"Help me," groaned the creature. Goodwin screamed, but a familiar hand clamped over her mouth.

Psyche grabbed Goodwin and, with surprising strength, pulled her to the ground. Goodwin could see her looking around frantically.

"What was–" Goodwin muttered around Psyche's hand.

"Shh!" hissed Psyche. The thunder and lightning had stopped, and the wind had slowed. Rain still dripped down from the trees, but it seemed that the storm had passed. Eventually, Psyche loosened her grip and Goodwin shook her off. She removed the hood from her rain jacket, looking around at the darkness, trying to get a bearing on where they were. She could hear and smell the lake, but she could not see it.

Goodwin took a few steps forward and tripped, nearly plummeting off a cliff. For the second time, Psyche grabbed her, grasping the back of her jacket and yanking her down. Goodwin kneeled in the mud, feeling it soak through her jeans.

They were on the lake shore, at the top of a steep washout. From the sound, Goodwin guessed they were high above the water. The rain had stopped, and the clouds dispersed, revealing a huge full moon.

Goodwin did not recognize this part of the lake. With a jolt, she realized that she had left her phone in the car. She had no idea what time it was. She didn't know how far they had walked—it could have been minutes or hours.

She tried to look around but all she could see was the lake before her, still churning from the storm.

Psyche stretched out a blackened hand, pointing to the lake.

Out of the darkness came the ghostly prow of a small boat. A dinghy, with a familiar shape. Goodwin's stomach dropped.

Psyche's strange, bony hand unfurled like a spider on her shoulder. Her touch was as cold as death, nearly weightless, but Goodwin found that she could not move. She was not uncomfortable in her paralysis; it was as if she was floating inside of herself, a mere spectator of the world around her. Her panic screamed to her like a voice in a well—present, but far, far away.

In the moon's blue light Goodwin could see the dinghy coming closer, buzzing through the still water. Goodwin strained to see who was driving. She saw a flash of red hair and at first she thought that it was Hunter Wellworth. Her heart leapt—maybe Hunter was looking for Amber's body, hoping to move it before the police searched the area.

But the person piloting the boat couldn't be Hunter. They had his flaming red hair and were driving Hunter's boat, but the driver was too small. Barely tall enough to see over the wheel.

As the dinghy slowed in front of them Goodwin realized that the person driving the boat was not Hunter, but his oldest son, Tanner. Tanner was too young to drive a boat, especially alone and at night. Goodwin wondered how he even navigated here in the dark.

Then she saw a bright light trailing through the water, just next to the prow of the boat. The light was a soft green, moving languidly below the surface of the lake. It was the same color as the faces in the trees, and Goodwin felt a harsh wave of dread.

The answer came to her. The light was a lure.

As Goodwin watched, the light stopped, and Tanner killed the engine of the small boat. He was close enough that she could have shouted to him, and in a wild panic she tried to do just that.

But Goodwin remained paralyzed. She could only watch helplessly as Tanner looked down into the darkened water, his face a pale disc above a bright orange life jacket.

"Amber?"

His voice, high with fear, echoed around the quiet lake. The ghostly light under the water had disappeared, and for a long moment there was nothing but silence.

Then came a soft voice. It was distorted, as if coming from deep underwater.

"Hey there, buddy."

"Amber!" called Tanner. "Amber, where are you? We've all been looking for you…"

There was a long, cold silence. Tanner leaned on the edge of the boat. He was crying. "We miss you, Amber, Ms. Gloria misses you. I didn't tell my parents, just like I promised…."

Again, silence. Goodwin recognized the voice of Amber as the same one in the woods who begged her to find her baby.

"A mimic," whispered Psyche

"Who was that?" Boomed a voice, different from the voice of Amber. This was a horrible sound, distorted, stretched, and deepened. The sweetness melted away, leaving behind the reality.

"What?" asked Tanner, his face pale with terror. "I don't see anyone. I came alone, I promise."

There was another long silence. Then: "Good." The voice of Amber, or something pretending to be Amber, returned.

"Where are you?" whispered Tanner. Goodwin could see fear changing his face. He had one hand on the wheel as if prepared to peel off at any moment.

The glowing light returned, slowly circling the boat before slipping around the side away from where Goodwin and Psyche crouched.

"I'm over here, Tanner. I'm in the water."

"Where? I don't see you" whined Tanner. He looked over the side of the small boat into the water, into the stirring light. He did not see the long black tendril that slipped up the side of the boat, as thick as a tap root and as fast as a snake.

Goodwin's mouth went dry as Tanner leaned further into the water, the opposite side of the boat rising against his weight. The tendril looped itself around Tanner's ankle. The voice, now returning to its natural tone, asked:

"Tanner, would you like to meet your brother?"

The movement was so fast that if Goodwin had not been enthralled she would have missed it. One moment, the chubby kid was staring into the water, and the next he was gone. His body was pulled off of the opposite side of the boat. Tanner's head cracked, face first, against the edge of the dinghy before he was flung into the water.

Tanner floated, limp and face down, his head cocked at an unnatural angle. Black blood was splattered on the inside of the boat, glittering in the moonlight. Then once more a tentacle reached up from the water. It wrapped itself carefully around Tanner's body and pulled him, lifejacket and all, under the surface of the lake.

The dinghy groaned. Thick tendrils wrapped around the boat like ropes, sliding over each other, slick and black like Goodwin's dream. It looked like an old scrimshaw of a Kraken eating a boat. There was a scream of metal as the craft was cleaved in two. It sank, disappearing into the lake depths with Tanner Wellworth.

Goodwin's vision began to tunnel. She felt, more than saw, Psyche leading her from the lake, back through the forest. Numbly she allowed herself to be pulled away, away from the horrors of the dark water.

CHAPTER FIFTEEN

GOODWIN JERKED AWAKE IN HER police cruiser.

She was back in the gravel lot near the dock where Dale and Jeff had gone missing. Spears of sunlight reached across the sky from the first break of dawn, cutting paths through the steam coming off of the water.

For a wild moment, Goodwin wondered if she had imagined the whole thing. Then she looked down at herself and saw that she was still wet and filthy from the storm, covered in mud from her knees down. She began to shiver—a mixture of her clammy clothes and the terror of what she had seen. The creature in the lake had killed Tanner Wellworth and then crushed his boat like a bath toy. It was too horrible to be real, but it must have been.

A half-memory rose to her mind—stumbling back through the woods, barely conscious, getting into her car while the face of Psyche, grinning like a Cheshire cat, floated before her.

Now that you know, you can never unknow.

The child of dark water will not stop until it destroys its creator.

Goodwin pressed her hands to her eyes. It wasn't possible. But she had seen it herself and couldn't blame this one on food poisoning. Unless she had a brain tumor or was otherwise mentally compromised, she could not doubt what she had seen. Something, pretending to be Amber, had lured Tanner Wellworth from his home. It had mimicked her voice, and it even appeared to make Tanner hallucinate. What did he see when the creature had called him to look in the water?

Do you want to meet your brother?

Remembering the voice from last night brought bile to her throat. That horrible, animal voice that came from somewhere much deeper than the bottom of the lake. That voice was something evil.

Poor Tanner. Goodwin rested her face in her hands. Another young life snuffed out right in front of her, and she hadn't been able to stop it. No one deserved to die like that, least of all a child. She could hear the hollow and sickening sound his skull made as it cracked against the boat. All that black blood pouring down the inside of the boat in the moonlight…

Goodwin thought of what Psyche had told her, about how a seed had been planted in the lake. A seed that turned into something malignant, a sentient creature that sought revenge from its creator and did so by taking what was closest to him. Her radio blatted shrilly, causing her to jump.

It was Sheriff Breeson.

"I'm going to need you down to the station, Officer. We have an urgent case."

Goodwin glanced at the electric clock on the dash. It was 5 am, well before her reporting time of 7 am. Normally, Sheriff Breeson was a stickler about shifts, claiming the department could not afford to pay overtime.

Goodwin had a pretty good idea of what it was about. But when she asked why he wanted her to come in early, her worst fears were confirmed. In a halting voice, Sheriff Breeson told her that the oldest Wellworth boy had gone missing, along with one of the family boats.

Goodwin agreed to come in early. She rushed home to change into her uniform, shamefully hiding her dirty clothes at the bottom of the hamper. The whole time her head swam guiltily. She knew what had happened to Tanner, but how could she tell anyone? Who would believe her? As she started the car, she wondered how she was going to convince her superior that a lake monster had eaten the missing boy.

CHAPTER SIXTEEN

THE TOWN OF RIDGEWAY WAS in an absolute panic.

The formerly sleepy hamlet became a nest of paranoia and fear overnight. People were locking their doors for the first time in decades, windows were kept closed and locked despite the sweltering heat. Children stopped playing in the streets, giving the town an eerie quiet. From the bar to the diner to the hardware store, everyone tittered about the strange disappearance of Tanner Wellworth.

From what Goodwin could gather during her hurried meals at Wranglers, almost everyone in Ridgeway believed the first part of the official story: that Tanner Wellworth had taken his parents' boat out at night and had gotten caught in the storm. In a lakeside community, this sort of thing was not unheard of.

It was the second part of the story– that Tanner had met with a terrible accident and drowned, that people couldn't stomach.

"Tanner Wellworth has been on boats since he was four years old," said Jim Weaver, "All the kids around here know basic boat safety. He would have never gone out without a life jacket, especially if the weather was bad."

"And why hasn't the boat turned up?" pondered Harold Spell. "The storm wasn't bad enough to sink a boat, and most of the lake out there isn't deep enough to hide a wreck."

"I'm telling you," replied Jim. "There is something bad in that water."

How right they all are, thought Goodwin.

The missing little boy had put enormous pressure on the police. Hunter Wellworth and his father, Grant, were with Sheriff Breeson every day. In the weeks following Tanner's disappearance, the Wellworth family had full control of police resources, as well as all the Search and Rescue teams from the county. These included search dogs, underwater sonar boats, and ground teams. The disappearances of Amber Prenley, Dale Kyler, and Jeff Wright were completely eclipsed by Tanner's disappearance.

Goodwin tried, both on the clock and off, to find the place Psyche had taken her– the washout above the lake where she had seen Tanner killed and taken by the creature. But she had no luck—the forest seemed to stretch on forever in every direction, and when she tried to follow the shoreline, she often found herself stopped by a fallen tree or impassable mass of pricker bushes. She considered trying to tell Sheriff Breeson, but a fever dream of walking through a forest with a witch and seeing a baby swamp monster was hardly evidence. He would probably drug-test her.

Goodwin's other police duties didn't give her much time to investigate on her own. The veneer of panic that covered Ridgeway had brought with it paranoia and suspicion. The hypervigilance of the townspeople had made policing harder, not easier.

While Sheriff Breeson was out riding around with the Wellworths, Goodwin responded to endless calls from spooked locals. Harold Spell had called about a shady man hanging around outside the hardware store, who turned out to be a contractor from the town over looking for a plumbing fitting. Wanda Sims had called three separate times, the first being when she saw a suspicious character lurking on her street, who was revealed to be a friend of her son Brendan. The second was the same, and the third was a hysterical late-night call about a man creeping around her backyard. When Goodwin rushed over to investigate, the "man" was revealed to be a black liquor store bag caught in the bushes.

Goodwin couldn't be mad at them. Their panic was appropriate if misdirected. Threat hung heavy over Ridgeway, as tangible as the humidity in the air. The lake was the lifeblood of these people, and it had been corrupted. The water itself had gone bad, spoiled in the summer heat. And all those people disappearing…any fool could tell that something was not right,

Ridgewood may not be an educated town, but its residents were sharp and sensitive to changes in the land. They knew that something had taken hold of their beloved Lake Munahegan, and it was picking them off one by one.

Goodwin knew all about it but couldn't do a damn thing.

Now that you know, you can never unknow

At night she paced the cool hardwood floors of the rental house, ignoring the grime accumulating on the bottom of her bare feet. She wasn't much of a housekeeper, and with all the overtime she had been working, the place was a disaster.

Goodwin had bought a whiteboard and hung it under a single light in the kitchen. There she wrote all the facts as she knew them. She used magnets to hang pictures of Amber Prenley, Dale Kyler, Jeff Wright, and now Tanner Wellworth. Her notes scrolled crazily across the white surface. She drained a multitude of pens. But she still felt no closer to figuring out how to end this. She looked at the picture of Amber, her blue eyes looking sadder by the day. Next to the picture she had written:

Hunter Wellworth– father of Amber's child

She had not proven this, despite best efforts. On a rare free afternoon Goodwin had interviewed all of Amber's school friends, and not one of them could name a boy she went with. But Goodwin knew that Amber had spent a lot of time around Hunter, and Goodwin saw him as the kind of creep that would knock up the teenage babysitter. It was assumptive but probably true.

She thought again about the visions Psyche had shown her. She shook her head. If someone in the police academy had told her that she would be basing her investigation on the visions of a shaman, she would have smacked them in the face.

Now here she was, frantically trying to find this "shaman." Psyche had disappeared, and though Goodwin had searched the area by the dock both alone and with a group, the woman had not turned up. It seemed that she had shown Goodwin all that she was willing to show. It was up to her to figure it out.

Goodwin had nightmares. It was always Amber's body wrapped in that blue tarp, heavily pregnant, chained to the bottom of the lake. She awoke from these dreams in a cold sweat, thinking of Gloria Prenley– at home and without answers as to what happened to her daughter and grandchild.

Goodwin guessed that Hunter had bought Amber's silence with the engagement ring, then lured Amber from her home, possibly promising her a moonlight ride on the lake. There he had subdued her, wrapped her in a tarp, weighed her down with chains, and thrown her overboard. Did he kill her before throwing her into the water? Maybe he didn't. Maybe he just hurt her enough to get her into the tarp and she drowned. The callousness of humans never ceased to amaze Goodwin.

Something Psyche said floated to her mind:

A seed has been planted in this place—

She thought of Amber's pregnant belly, slit open in a horrible underwater c-section. Had she been alive for that? The blood glittering under the full moon danced in her mind, the slimy creature being birthed from some other world into ours.

Goodwin looked at the pictures of Dale and Jeff. How did they factor into this? They were fishing when they went missing—Goodwin herself had seen the cooler and chairs, the lines dropped in the water. Perhaps they were in the wrong place at the wrong time. Drunk and fishing in the dark, they would be easy to trick.

And now Tanner Wellworth was gone, lured into the lake and killed.

It chooses its victims to spite its creator.

"It certainly does," groaned Goodwin.

CHAPTER SEVENTEEN

HUNTER WELLWORTH WAS COMING UNDONE.

Everything had changed since the morning he heard his wife scream from Tanner's empty bedroom. It was as if all the shadows in Hunter's life had grown long. At first, he tried to keep up appearances. He was too shell-shocked to do any work, but he kept going to the bank, wearing his suit and tie. It was magical thinking: if he behaved as if nothing was wrong, Tanner would return home, and life would resume.

What Hunter was experiencing now was not life, it was purgatory. At the bank, he alternated between pacing his office and staring out of the window, gazing down at the city of Ridgeway, wondering who took his son and why.

Hunter never believed that Tanner had taken the boat out and drowned. Tanner, like his father, had been driving boats since he was old enough to stand up. He would have never taken the dinghy out at night—it had no lights. He especially would not have gone out during a storm. And even *if* Tanner had taken the boat, he always wore his life jacket. He would have been able to swim ashore if something had happened.

No, Hunter was convinced someone had taken his son. He believed that the missing dinghy was a red herring. He tried in vain to get his theory out—when he wasn't on the phone with the cops, he was talking to his daddy, demanding that Grant increase the pressure on local authorities.

They all looked at him with the same pitying expression. The look you give a hysterical parent who is unable to handle the truth.

When pacing the office wasn't enough, Hunter took to walking the streets. He looked rabid in his wrinkled suit, red-eyed in the shimmering heat. He stumbled up and down the streets of Ridgeway like a sleepwalker, wandering from one end of the town to the other. People who used to kiss Hunter Wellworth's ass now politely averted their gaze as he stumbled through town.

This came to a head one sunny afternoon when Hunter spotted a little boy who looked like Tanner walking down the street. He had bright red hair and was wearing an enormous shirt. He was holding hands with a lanky, tall man with thick tattooed arms and long hair.

Hunter screamed. He ran forward and smashed the long-haired man over the head with the corner of his briefcase.

"Tanner!" he howled, grabbing the boy by the back and spinning him around to face him, his heart hammering with wild hope. But it was not Tanner, it was a young woman with a short haircut in a tee-shirt dress.

"Get the fuck off of me!" she screamed, clawing at Hunter's face. "You hit my husband!" She shoved Hunter away and fell to the ground to crawl towards the tall man, who was holding his head and groaning, blood pouring down his face.

The couple had pressed charges and once more Grant Wellworth had sprung into action. Wheels were greased, threats were made, and ultimately the whole thing disappeared. After that Grant insisted that Hunter stay away from the bank, just until he was "feeling better."

Staying at home was worse for Hunter. People drifted in and out of the lakeside home like shades—police officers, coworkers from the bank, family members. It was as if they all existed in a dream, one interaction running into the next. People brought flowers, casseroles, cookies. These gifts sat in a moldering pile by the door, filling the air with flies.

Tabitha had taken a break from her diet of sedatives long enough to pack up Jay and leave for her mother's place. In a way, Hunter was grateful that they were gone. He couldn't stand the way Tabitha looked at him, red eyes like pools of resentment. Tabby never outright accused Hunter of driving Tanner away because she didn't have to.

Hunter spent as much time as possible searching for his son. It became his sole focus, a drive beyond obsession. He sent lists of sex offenders in the area to the police to interview, he searched the woods around the lake house, and though he did not believe the missing boat theory, Hunter covered his dining room table with a large map of the lake to be grid searched. Hunter participated in all of the official search parties, though his father had started to accompany him at Sheriff Breeson's suggestion. Hunter's erratic behavior made the cops nervous.

No expense had been spared in the search for Tanner Wellworth. His MISSING posters covered the town, plastered over the faded posters for Dale Kyler, Jeff Wright, and Amber Prenley.

Grant Wellworth had also pulled some strings to get the state police's underwater sonar, as well as a limnologist to create a map of the lake currents to estimate the drift of the dingy. The cops had done a thorough comb of the violent criminals in the town, of which there were few, and anyone who had gotten so much as a traffic ticket in the past year had been questioned by either Officer Goodwin or Sheriff Breeson.

It had been exactly twenty-three days since they had first discovered Tanner missing from his bed, and they still had no idea where he had gone.

Hunter stood alone on the prow of his father's yacht, watching the sonar search yet another cove on the coast of the lake. The cops swarmed the boats as divers bobbed in and out of the water like seals, carrying heavy pieces of sonar tech. The lake smelled less bad in this area, somehow protected from the strange bacteria bloom taking place near Ridgeway. Hunter stood under the blazing sun, staring listlessly into the water.

"Gonna get a sunburn, son." Grant's voice came from behind him. Grant Wellworth was a small, neat man. Despite the situation and the heat of the day, Grant Wellworth remained cool. He was dressed for a day on the water, wearing a pastel polo, khaki shorts, and boat shoes. In his hand he held a gin and tonic.

Grant gently guided his son to the shaded captain's cabin. He tried to hand him a drink but Hunter didn't take it. He was like a zombie, lost in death, still staring at the lake.

"This is bad business," sighed Grant, shaking his head.

"The Wellworths have lived in Ridgeway for decades and nothing like this has happened before. I just can't understand it. The lake is spoiled, those two men disappeared, poor Gloria Prenley losing her girl Amber, and now Tanner…"

Hunter abruptly turned on his father. With his red eyes and inflamed skin, he looked like a man in hell.

"Don't you dare lump my son in with Amber Prenley!" he screamed. "Tanner is not a knocked up redneck slut! Tanner is a little boy! My first born and your grandson!" Hunter's jagged voice echoed across the lake, causing a few of the police officers to look over.

"None of this is my fault!" Hunter gasped.

There was a deafening silence.

"No one said it was your fault" replied Grant calmly. The two men stared at each other, and a look of recognition flashed across Grant's eyes. Grant Wellworth was a shrewd and calculating man, and he knew Hunter better than anyone. As soon as Grant mentioned Amber Prenley, he saw something behind his son's eyes, something that Grant recognized.

Guilt.

"It's all right, Hunter," said Grant soothingly, grabbing Hunter by the arm. "It's all right. Whatever happened here…we will get it sorted. Let's just focus on finding Tanner, okay?"

But Hunter wasn't listening.

The cops on the lake were used to outbursts from the families of missing persons, and if they noticed Hunter's yelling, they had already gone back to work.

All except one.

Officer Alice Goodwin stood on a small police boat less than half a mile from the yacht. She glared at Hunter, her burns pink in the saturated sunlight, her gray eyes shimmering from under her police baseball cap. As they stared at each other, a lump rose in Hunter's throat. It felt like a noose around his neck.

CHAPTER EIGHTEEN

BETWEEN THE CONSTANT CALLS FROM townsfolk and the searches for Tanner Wellworth, Goodwin did not have a lot of time to work on her own theories about the lake creature.

However, all the time on the water helped her think about it. She remembered how the creature had mimicked Amber's voice, how it could make people hallucinate. But it was not some sort of magical spirit. It was a physical thing with mass. She had seen it with her own eyes, seen its slick, octopus-like appendage grab Tanner's leg.

She guessed that it was most active at night, and like all nocturnal animals, the creature probably had some sort of den. A place where it could hide out during the day. Goodwin figured that the most likely spot was where Dale Kyler and Jeff Wright had disappeared, the area down by the old, busted dock.

That spot seemed to have gotten the worst of the so-called "bacteria bloom." It made sense in a way—that was a quiet part of the lake, a place both deep and undisturbed. The locals had told Goodwin that, while the dock had been a popular fishing spot, it had fallen out of favor since the new dock was built six years ago. Only a few locals fished there now; it was the kind of place you had to know about to find.

Which made it an excellent spot to dump a body.

At night, Goodwin was plagued by dreams.

She was back at Amber's watery grave, the home of the beast. It covered the lake floor, a great, writhing mass of blackness like thousands of huge worms. In the center was Amber's body, still shrouded by the blue tarp, pulsing like a great cancerous heart.

Amber's body was no longer alone. Now there were three bodies tethered to the lake bottom. Each was wrapped in a black film that reminded Goodwin of cling wrap, connected to the great mass by ropey lines like black umbilical cords. Goodwin could make out a tuft of bright orange hair hanging out of one of the blackened pods. Somehow Goodwin knew that the bodies were being drained—absorbed by this eldritch creature that spewed filth and consumed so hatefully.

Goodwin awoke from one of these dreams with a gasp.

Drenched in a cold sweat, Goodwin got to her feet, pacing her bedroom floor in the dark. Psyche had told her that the creature chooses its victims to spite its creator, but she had said something else too.

Once it has discovered what will hurt its creator the most, it uses it as bait.

Bait. Goodwin furrowed her brow, thinking about the choice of word. Bait implies more than a tormentor. *Bait* implied a hunt. *This creature killed Tanner and is now going to use him as bait to destroy its creator.*

Outside, a cold moon shone on the sleeping woods. Goodwin had a sudden sense of dread. Wasn't it a full moon when Tanner had been taken?

See the creature bloom in the fullness of the moon…

Before she could talk herself out of it, Goodwin put on an old pair of jeans and a shirt, grabbing her gun, her badge, and her flashlight. She got into her cruiser and headed out to the old fishing dock.

CHAPTER NINETEEN

HUNTER SAT ON HIS BACK lawn, staring out at the darkened lake. Of course, the searches had turned up nothing in the lake. There was nothing there to find. Someone had taken his son, his family, his legacy, his life. He sat in the grass by the dock, drinking out of the bottle. A full moon winked at him between swigs.

Behind Hunter the lake house was dark and empty, a monument to loneliness. Hunter couldn't bring himself to be angry at Tabitha and Jay for abandoning him at his darkest hour. His father had suggested punishing her with a brutal divorce and custody battle, but Hunter found he simply did not care. Without the heir to Wellworth legacy, there seemed no point in keeping the facade. Tabitha and Jay were useless to him now.

The family was gone, and the visitors stopped coming by. But the lake house was not empty.

Ever since Tanner's disappearance, Hunter had been sleeping in his son's room, cramming his body into the boy's twin bed, as if keeping it warm for his safe return.

The past few nights he heard someone—something—walking slowly up and down the halls. It had a rotting smell, and an odd dragging gait, as if pulling something along with it. Hunter could see strange lights under the door as the creature tapped at the walls and rattled the doorknob.

It laughed at him.

The moon rose higher, the water lapped; his son stayed gone. Hunter began to cry, the kind of choking sobs one does in private. He knew that he wasn't going to find his son. He knew, deep in his heart, that whatever had taken Tanner had no intention of returning him, dead or alive.

He would have to live his life not knowing, just like Gloria Prenley.

It was a horrible thing, to wish you could find your child's dead body. It was horrible to see death as a best-case scenario, but not knowing was worse. The questions fluttered in his face like insects—what happened to Tanner? Where was he? Was he alive? Was he being kept somewhere? It was all too much; too many unknowns that burned into Hunter like a hot brand.

Losing a child was devastating. Not knowing was intolerable.

Hunter fell to his knees in the thick grass of the lawn that sloped to the lake.

"Just do it!" he screamed into the black water. "Just kill me! Just kill me so I can be with my boy."

The moon blinked, the water rippled, and aside from the echo of his own voice, silence filled the air. Hunter collapsed into the tall grass, sobbing.

"Come find me, Daddy."

Tanner's voice, unmistakable to his father, slithered through the grass. Hunter jumped to his feet, stumbling with drunken effort.

"Tanner?" he gasped.

"Please come get me...I'm so cold..."

The voice was coming from off the lake, just around the corner of the forest and out of sight. Hunter did not consider how this was possible. He ran towards the dock, tripping over the bottle of whiskey in the grass.

He fumbled with the keys of his fishing boat, a small craft with a high-quality motor and a light for night fishing. It was the same boat that he and Amber had used so many times, the boat that had carried her to her final resting place.

"Come... find me..."

Hunter fired the engine, not bothering with a life jacket. "I'm coming Tanner, I'm coming, baby."

Hunter revved the boat. He pointed the nose of the craft towards the sound of his son's voice. But he did not need navigation or the boat's light.

The moon was bright, and Hunter knew where the voice was coming from. If he wanted to see his son, he would have to visit Amber Prenley.

CHAPTER TWENTY

GOODWIN CHEWED HER NAILS AS she drove towards the old dock. It was a bad habit she had thought she'd broken. She tried to identify what was making her so jumpy. Everything on the country road— every shadow, every darting animal—seemed to be a threat. It was as if the whole landscape was transformed into a beast by the moon. It lit the way like a cold, pale face, a death mask in the velvet sky.

As Goodwin swung her cruiser into the gravel lot she realized what she felt. She was afraid. Not just afraid: Officer Alice Goodwin was scared shitless, and she wanted to run away.

This was new for her. She had always been the kind of person to jump in when she was needed, to throw self-preservation to the wind. And what had that loyalty gotten her? Absently, she touched her burned face, her ruined ear. For the first time, she considered abandoning the whole thing. This was beyond the scope of the police.

What was the thing in the lake? How did a young girl's pregnant body turn into a monster? Goodwin could not explain it, she didn't have words for such an abomination. And now it was as if the creature was part of her, haunting her waking life and filling her dreams with slick black tentacles and screaming faces of the drowned dead.

"This lake is a fertile place."

Goodwin parked the cruiser. She tried to come to terms with the situation. She was convinced Amber and her unborn child, through the process of being killed and thrown into the lake by the child's father, had transformed. Amber's corpse and that of her unborn fetus were no longer just lifeless bodies, rotting in a watery grave. They had become a single, powerful and malevolent creature.

It had been created through malice, thrown into the water to avoid the yoke of responsibility, of gossip, of inconvenience. This creature wanted to punish the situation that created it, it wanted to destroy the town, to destroy Hunter Wellworth.

It wanted revenge on the creator that brought it into the world so carelessly.

"Don't we all." Groaned Goodwin. She knew she couldn't leave. From the moment Goodwin saw those pictures of Amber in Gloria's house, a connection had formed. Goodwin could not just walk away– not when she knew what had happened to Amber. She could not allow Gloria to suffer her kin becoming a monster.

She grabbed her flashlight and gun, stepping out of the cruiser into the hot, dark night.

The smell of rot was overpowering. Goodwin had been in several county morgues throughout her career, and the smell coming off the water was similar. She turned on her flashlight and then remembered Psyche's warning about the creature being able to see it. She turned it off, allowing her eyes to adjust to the blue moonlight. The shore lapped, and the forest was quiet as Goodwin started to walk through the path in the woods.

She had no idea what she was looking for but felt driven by an unseen force. She stuck to the bank of the lake as the moon glinted off the water.

There was a rumbling sound, like the turning of earth. Goodwin froze with fear.

Something was watching her. And it was not human. Nothing human could make her feel like that. It was as if icy fingers were touching the back of her neck. She stood in animal paralysis. Around her the forest was quiet. No nightbird calls, no snapping of twigs.

Goodwin forced herself to keep going. She hunkered low, moving from tree trunk to tree trunk until she rounded a corner. She looked down at a knot of tree roots like gnarled fingers in the muck of the lake and had a flash of recognition. This was where she had found Dale Kyler's lighter.

A loud noise broke the quiet of the night. A distant purring of a boat engine. Goodwin recognized it as a small craft, barely more than a rowboat. Instinctively she ducked down. Through the veil of trees she could see a small boat purring along the moonlit water.

"Tanner!" A familiar man's voice split the night air. As the craft got closer Goodwin could see it was Hunter Wellworth, his red hair almost incandescent in the moonlight. He was screaming his son's name, slurring.

And another voice: "Come find me daddy… I am lost and scared…"

Goodwin's heart dropped. She heard the voice as clear as day, and she knew that Hunter had heard the voice of his child, calling him further and further into the lake.

But it was no child. Goodwin was not under the creature's glamor. She heard its real voice, the voice that belched out of flaps in the thick black skin, the horrible voice that was low and distorted, a mockery of human speech. *Bait.*

She watched as Hunter zoomed towards the dilapidated dock, skidding erratically across the lake's black surface.

"I'm coming, Tanner!" He screamed.

As the boat zipped past her Goodwin could have sworn she heard a low giggle.

Goodwin ran towards the dock, tripping and fumbling over roots that did not seem to be there before. One snagged her foot. She fell to the ground and the roots wrapped around her as quickly as snakes.

A small voice spoke directly into her good ear as the roots pulled her into a vise-like grip:

"I am going to kill you all."

Goodwin gathered her strength and yanked herself up, snapping away twigs and branches, running towards the dock. She stumbled into the gravel clearing just in time to see Hunter Wellworth. His boat was anchored a short way from the end of the dock. He had a long pole and appeared to be frantically probing the bottom of the lake.

"GIVE ME MY SON BACK!" Hunter jabbed the pole into the lake like a spear.

He looked insane. Even from a distance, Goodwin could see his fevered eyes, his tear-stained cheeks, his slobbering mouth. Goodwin knew it was a bad idea to approach this man alone.

She crept back to her cruiser, hidden in the cover of trees. Goodwin made the decision to call for backup, she'd take the heat and the questions later. The town was swarming with state cops. Even if Sheriff Breeson wanted to turn a blind eye to Hunter's suspicious behavior, the state police may say otherwise.

After she radioed in, she began to approach the dock. The creature was still in the lake, and Hunter Wellworth was in its trap. With one hand gently resting on the butt of her gun, Goodwin carefully made her way down the dock.

Hunter didn't see her until she spoke.

"Odd time of night to be searching the lake."

Hunter turned and looked at her, less than twelve feet from his boat. He didn't seem to see her—his wild hair and burning eyes made him look like a flaming skull. He stumbled towards her, obviously drunk, the boat swaying on the water.

"You!" he screamed. "You did this! This all started because of you!"

"Amber Prenley did not go missing because of me," snarled Goodwin.

"WHO GIVES A SHIT ABOUT AMBER PRENLEY?"

"I do," She shone her flashlight in Hunter's face, "And I think that you were the father of her child. I think that's why you killed her and threw her in the lake, in this very spot. Isn't that right?"

Hunter stared at her agape. "How…how could you…"

"Hunter Wellworth, I have reason to believe that you are in grave danger. You need to come into the station for questioning—right now."

For a moment Hunter looked like he might consider it. Goodwin could see the flicker of morality behind his eyes.

Then it went out.

"What proof do you have?" growled Hunter, baring his teeth, "And who the fuck do you think you are talking to? The Wellworths have owned the cops in Ridgeway for years."

Hunter Wellworth produced a small gun from the waistband of his stained shorts. He pointed it at Goodwin. Goodwin tried to keep her heartbeat slow, keep him talking, and stall for time.

The creature had other ideas.

"So what if I *did* kill Amber Prenley?" The water around Hunter's boat began to churn. "Amber Prenley was a nobody! She was nothing! She was garbage!"

"Hunter Wellworth, you are aiming a weapon at a police officer. Put the gun down."

"NO!" Hunter screamed, eyes rolling, "NO! My son is here, and I am going to find him, I am going to—"

"Daddy…"

Both turned to the source of the sound.

Something emerged slowly from the black water, twisting up in an unnatural motion. Though both saw it, but only Hunter was under the creature's glamor.

Hunter Wellworth saw his son, Tanner. He was smiling, happy, and very much alive. He was floating just above the fetid water, the soles of his boat shoes touching its shimmering surface.

Tanner walked on water like Jesus Christ himself, coming back to return glory to the Wellworth home. He opened his arms to his father.

"Daddy, you came back for me."

Hunter could not hear Goodwin's screams. She saw the truth.

A black tendril was holding aloft what was left of Tanner's decomposing body. It puppetted the body to and fro, causing the skeletal arms to sway and the limp head to flop side to side. Tanner's eyes were gone, empty black sockets in gray flesh. His red hair clung to his scalp in patches. He was still wearing a life vest, but the lower half of Tanner's body was gone. Tanner's torso dangled greenish viscera, eaten away by animals, and bloated with rot. As Goodwin watched, a piece of Tanner's flesh detached from his arm. It hung briefly by a strip of blackened tendon before falling into the water with a plop.

Goodwin screamed for Hunter to not go in the water, but it was too late. Hunter threw his gun aside and dove into the blackness, began paddling wildly towards the body of his son.

With violent swiftness, Hunter was snatched from the water, held aloft by his leg. He hung upside down, his shirt pulled up to expose white stomach as Hunter coughed and gasped, lungs full of thick water.

The guttural sound of Hunter's choking knocked Goodwin out of her trance. She aimed her weapon at the long black appendage but couldn't get a good shot as it writhed in the moonlight.

The surrounding water had become alive with snake-like masses reaching up and wrapping around the small boat. Hunter finally unclogged his lungs. He screamed and screamed, not a horror movie scream but a high-pitched animal sound, like a rabbit in a trap.

Goodwin tried to take aim, her arms trembling, but an appendage swung at her, knocking her to the ground hard enough to crack the planks. Her gun skittered away and fell into the lake. She struggled to get to her feet but froze when she saw Hunter framed in the moonlight.

The creature had slid Hunter through its tentacles, turning him upright so he could better view the spectacle. A large bud slithered up to Hunter Wellworth, getting inches from his terrified face. The bud bulged like a hellish lily, layers of slick wet plant matter peeling back to reveal dripping flesh as the voice came from the deep.

"Father…"

"No." groaned Hunter, "no, no this can't be."

It was the face of his dead child. Not Tanner, but the baby he had with Amber. The baby that was so soon going to enter the world. Its eyes were full of mud.

With great effort Goodwin got up, taking a few painful steps before she felt something tighten on her ankle. With a fierce jerk, her feet were knocked out from under her, and she fell to the dock again, white-hot pain shooting up her elbow. Something was definitely broken. The pain paralyzed her.

"Something precious," whispered the lake. Hunter's eyes bulged. His face turned red. The slithering tentacles were contracting like a boa constrictor. As the baby's face retreated into the water, another stalk took its place, rising up in the moonlight to be seen.

The creature dangled the rotten, mutilated body of Tanner in front of Hunter. This time the glamor was stripped away. In his dying moments,

Hunter Wellworth had to look at the destroyed carcass of the only thing he loved in this world.

Another appendage grabbed Goodwin's wrist and began yanking her towards the edge of the dock. In a panic, Goodwin grasped onto one of the dock posts, agony radiating from her shoulder. She struggled against the impossible strength of the creature just long enough to see a tentacle wrap around Hunter's throat.

The lake emitted a gurgling laugh.

In a single, easy motion the creature ripped off Hunter Wellworth's head. His decapitated body danced wildly as blood poured from the stump of his neck like a geyser. That was the last thing Goodwin saw before being yanked into the black water.

The sludge was overpowering. She struggled but her shoulder was broken and singing with pain. She was no match for the strong appendages that wrapped around her, pulling her down to the bottom. Filthy water filled her mouth and nose with the smell of rot. She felt herself being wrapped in something thick and slimy, and then she felt no more.

CHAPTER TWENTY-ONE

ALICE GOODWIN WAS SOMEWHERE SOFT, and bright. For the first time in a long time, Alice felt safe. She felt no fear or pain. She opened her eyes and before her was a young woman. She had flowing auburn hair and was wearing a sundress. She had her back to Goodwin, cradling something in her arms. Goodwin could hear her singing a lullaby. She also heard something else.

The happy giggle of an infant.

The girl turned, and Goodwin saw the unmistakable pool-blue eyes of Amber Prenley. She was smiling, her face a halo of light. She looked beautiful. In her arms was a small bundle.

"It's all right now."

Goodwin was already forgetting that there was somewhere before this place. She was ready to leave behind the world of pain and fear. But something yanked on Goodwin's stomach, pulling her away. She didn't want to leave. She wanted to stay here with Amber Prenley, in this warm, soft place.

The force on her stomach yanked again, like a seatbelt in an accident. Goodwin stared pleadingly at Amber and, as if reading her mind, Amber sadly shook her head. No, she could not stay here.

Goodwin let the force pull her away. Before she left, Amber held up the bundle in her arms, and Alice saw the face of a baby boy. He had his mother's blue eyes.

CHAPTER TWENTY-TWO

GOODWIN WAS COCOONED AT THE bottom of the lake, wrapped in the tendrils of the creature. Forever stuck in a slick black pod, pulsing slightly, with all the other bodies around her. Soon she would be nothing but a skeleton. Then crushed to dust as the creature of the lake grew stronger and fed off of more victims.

A thick tendril slid past, led by a hideous, grinning human face. The tendril whipped around like a snake and Goodwin was staring at Hunter Wellworth's death mask, pulled into a terrible rictus smile.

Goodwin woke up screaming.

A waning moon loomed through the open window in the hospital room. She tried to sit up, forgetting for a moment the elaborate cast around her shoulder and yelping in pain. She had been in the hospital for three days. Ever since Hunter Wellworth had tried to kill her.

That was the story, anyway. The one that Goodwin repeated when she woke up. She told endless reporters and state officers that she had gone out to the dock to do some late-night searching. While she was there she had found Hunter Wellworth rooting in the water and behaving strangely. When confronted, Hunter attacked her and threw her into the lake. He believed Goodwin was dead and, fearing the consequences of killing a police officer, shot himself.

The story had holes—ones that Sheriff Breeson initially attempted to punch through. Had she known Hunter Wellworth was going to be there?

Why wasn't she in uniform? Why did Hunter's gun, found on the lake bottom, still have all its bullets?

But after Goodwin was taken to the hospital, bodies started to appear where she had been found. One by one they emerged from the bottom of the lake. First was Tanner Wellworth, decomposed almost beyond recognition. Then there was Jeff Wright, and less than a day later Dale Kyler washed ashore.

Amber Prenley and the remains of her unborn baby came up last.

The bodies were taken to the basement morgue of the hospital to be autopsied. With the exception of Tanner Wellworth, the bodies appeared to have sunk deep in the lakebed. Wrapped in layers of mud, the corpses had been mummified.

The coroner, a woman in her forties with black hair named Dr. Johanson, visited Goodwin in the hospital to see if she had an explanation.

"Sometimes the mud keeps 'em," said Dr. Johanson. "But I never seen something like this. It's as if they've been sucked dry, but underwater. It's very strange."

Goodwin wasn't much help to her. She didn't even know how she had gotten from the bottom of the lake to the shore where the state cops had found her.

The State police had taken over the Ridgeway Police Department. Through gossip brought in with hot meals from the Wrangler diner, Goodwin discovered that state investigators had done DNA testing on Amber's child, which definitively proved that Hunter Wellworth was the father.

After that fact came to light, Sheriff Breeson was proven too biased to be near the case. He had been shoved out on early retirement.

Goodwin was relieved that Hunter was finally caught, though the victory was joyless. No one would ever know what really happened that night on the lake dock. No one would know about the creature at the bottom of the lake. Was it still there, biding its time to kill again?

Only Goodwin knew of the true terror that lay below the surface. In that knowledge she was alone.

"Not completely alone."

Goodwin stifled her surprise. Psyche was sitting in her fourth story hospital window, casually dangling one dirty foot towards the floor, silhouetted by the moonlight.

"You….you pulled me out of the lake."

"Yes. But by the time I got there, the creature was already retreating. I just pulled you to shore."

"Is it gone?" whispered Goodwin.

Psyche nodded, silver teeth glinting in the dark.

"But how?"

"You broke the spell." Psyche's mouth didn't move when she spoke. The sound of her voice came from all around Goodwin. She could even hear it in her bad ear.

"You see, many people believe that magic is like science—put exact ingredients in, get something out. It isn't like that. Magic doesn't abide by any formula; magic is chaotic. It springs up out of nowhere and disappears just as fast and destructive as a tornado. That awful man didn't know what he was doing, he was just committing an evil act. But magic happens by accident all the time. You kill someone over here, you fuck someone over there, and sometimes all the chips fall into place. When that happens, nothing can be done to stop it. Except, somehow, you did."

Psyche locked eyes with Goodwin,

"You broke the spell. I don't know how, but you interrupted the process. The creature is gone. The human souls it held captive are set free."

"So the town is safe?"

"Safety is an illusion." Psyche grinned wider. "But they are under no current threat."

Goodwin closed her eyes and found warm tears of relief streaming down her face. Ridgeway was safe, the creature was gone, and Amber and her baby were finally at peace.

"You can rest now, Officer," said Psyche.

"I'm not an Officer anymore." Goodwin half-chuckled. "You can call me Alice."

"You may not be part of the law anymore, but you are a protector, Alice Goodwin." Psyche's eyes flashed in the moonlight as she spoke, "And there is always work for protectors in the world of magic. Perhaps we will meet again."

Goodwin's eyelids became very heavy. In between slow blinks Psyche disappeared from her window, but her voice stayed with Goodwin like a scent in the air.

"Go to sleep, Alice Goodwin. Go to sleep and dream of nothing."

She did.

EPILOGUE

WHEN GOODWIN FIRST ARRIVED AT Ridgeway, she felt that she would never belong. Now she felt that she could never leave.

She was also bound by the slowness of her recovery. During the fight she had broken her shoulder and fractured a femur. But worse than that, the oxygen deprivation in the lake had caused her to develop grand mal seizures. She was officially disabled in the line of duty, unable to continue her law enforcement career even if she had wanted to.

At least money would not be a concern. The day she was released from the hospital, Goodwin met a reedy man in an expensive suit waiting for her in the parking lot. He told her that he represented Grant Wellworth, who was willing to hand over a considerable sum of money in return for Goodwin agreeing to not sue the family.

The trust wasn't enough for Goodwin to retire, not even in Ridgeway. But the regular payments from the trust, along with her disability pay from the police force, was enough for Goodwin to get by for a while.

The whole town had come out for all three funerals. Dale Kyler and Jeff Wright had been buried in their family plots at Ridgeway cemetery. Amber Prenley and her child had an elaborate funeral that ended in a plot shrouded with flowers. Goodwin figured the town must have bought out every florist in the area.

Rumor had the Wellworth family paid for the whole thing.

Gloria Prenley finally got her answer, but was too heartbroken to stay in Ridgeway. She also received a settlement from the Wellworth Estate and used hers to flee to Florida. She didn't even unpack her house—just locked it up and left it to rot.

Hunter and Tanner's funerals had been private and out of state. No one in Ridgeway talked about the Wellworth family anymore. The fact that the manager at their local bank had killed five people, two of which were his own children, was too much for the community to bear. Better to treat it like an old photo album, boxed up and put away, something that could be remembered but never would.

Sheriff Breeson did not get to golf with Grant Wellworth in his retirement. After the news broke, the Wellworths had quietly sold the bank, packed up the family properties, and left. For the first time in decades, the Wellworth lake houses stood empty and haunted as castle ruins.

As for Alice Goodwin, things had started to look up. Everyone knew she had broken the case, and overnight she was something of a celebrity among the residents of Ridgeway. She was a welcome regular at the Wrangler Diner, where everyone knew her by name, and no one stared at her burns or the new surgical scars across her shoulder. Her house was paid up for the next few months, and her representative from the police union said her insurance would cover a seizure-detecting dog. Goodwin had wanted a dog since she was a little girl but was always too busy working. Not anymore.

In the evening Goodwin liked to go to the lake. Not the old dock where the bodies had been found, but the one in town where kids caught rainbow trout and teenagers went to hook up in the dark. There, among the laughter and bickering, Goodwin watched the sunset, throwing fantastic light across the clean and sweet-smelling water.

"You're a protector, and there is always work for a protector in the world of magic." Goodwin shook her head. It didn't seem so crazy anymore, not after the creature she had seen in the lake. Maybe other places could create such monsters. So-called fertile places, where creatures push through a doorway from their world into ours. Who would those people turn to for help with their problem? Who would believe such a thing in today's rational world, and want to help them?

"Me," whispered Goodwin.

CASTLE BRIDGE MEDIA RECOMMENDS...

If you liked this book, you might also enjoy reading the following titles from Castle Bridge Media available on Amazon or by order at your favorite book store:

ANIMAL CHARMER
Animal Charmer
By Rain Nox
Magic & Melody
By Rain Nox

Austinites
By In Churl Yo

Bloodsucker City
By Jim Towns

The Burning Gem
By Don Sawyer

THE CASTLE OF HORROR ANTHOLOGY SERIES
Volume 1
Volume 2: Holiday Horrors
Volume 3: Scary Summer
   Stories
Volume 4: Women Running
   From Houses
Volume 5: Thinly Veiled:
   The 70s
Volume 6: Femme Fatales*
Volume 7: Love Gone Wrong
Volume 8: Thinly Veiled:
   The 80s
Volume 9: Young Adult
Volume 10: Thinly Veiled:
   Saturday Mournings
Volume 11: Revenge
Edited By Jason Henderson
and In Churl Yo
*Edited By P.J. Hoover

Castle of Horror Podcast Book of Great Horror
Edited By Jason Henderson

Cherry Dark
By R.L. Wilburn

Child of Dark Water
By E.G. Rand

Dream State
By Martin Ott

Dominic
By Lee Guzman

FRENCH DECEPTION
A Forgery in Paris
By Janice Nagourney
A Forgery in Lyon
By Janice Nagourney
A Forgery in Marseille
By Janice Nagourney

FuturePast Sci-Fi Anthology
Edited by In Churl Yo

GLAZIER'S GAP
Ghosts of the Forbidden
By Leanna Renee Hieber

Hellfall
By Jay Gould

Isonation
By In Churl Yo

JAYU CITY CHRONICLES
The Hermes Protocol
By Chris M. Arnone
Necropolis Alpha
By Chris M. Arnone

Junk Film: Why Bad Movies Matter
By Katharine Coldiron

MID-LIFE CRISIS THRILLERS
18 Miles From Town
By Jason Henderson
Lost Angel
By Sam Knight
Ties That Kill
By Deven Greene

Nightwalkers: Gothic Horror Movies
By Bruce Lanier Wright

THE PATH
The Blue-Spangled Blue
By David Bowles
The Deepest Green
By David Bowles

St. Damned
By Ty Drago

SURF MYSTIC
Night of the Book Man
By Peyton Douglas
Dark of the Curl
By Peyton Douglas

The 23rd Hero
By Rebecca Anne Nguyen

The Thing That Happened When We Were Little
By Caroline Kelly Franklin

Vinyl Wonderland
By Mark Rigney

Yesterday's Tomorrows: The Golden Age of Science Fiction Movies
By Bruce Lanier Wright

Please remember to leave us your reviews on Amazon and Goodreads!
THANK YOU FOR SUPPORTING INDEPENDENT PUBLISHERS AND AUTHORS!
castlebridgemedia.com